Summer Heat

4M Ranch, Book 1

Debra Fisk

Royal Bee Publishing

Printed in the United States of America
First Printing: November 2016

Paperback ISBN: 978-0-9983435-0-1
Digital ISBN: 978-0-9983435-1-8

For my little Desire, who stayed by my side until this book was finished. Rest in peace, little girl. You will be forever in my heart.

"You gonna pour the coffee, young lady, or stand there like a statue?"

With the pot hovering above the cup, Misty Summers shook out of her frozen position and smiled at Wendell, one of the regulars at the counter. "Sorry." As the hot liquid sloshed into the mug, her eyes panned the room, troubled by the news she'd received earlier.

For a steamy late July Tuesday, the early morning breakfast crowd jammed into the Wrong Way Diner. She had served endless cups of coffee even though the broken air conditioner pushed the thermometer near ninety-five degrees, yet no one seemed to mind. *Where the heck is Carly?* Her best friend and coworker was habitually late.

"Wait— What are you doing?" Wendell croaked. The

elderly man placed his hand over hers and turned the pot upright to stop the overflow. Startled, she reached into the pocket of her apron, pulled out a small towel, and wiped up the puddle around his mug.

"I'm not with it this morning," she mumbled. July in Texas without air conditioning and a weight of personal problems fogged her brain. *Stay focused.* There were customers to wait on.

"Two specials up," the cook called from the kitchen. Misty scurried over to snatch the plates, placed them on a tray, and then delivered them to the table of tourists. The San Antonio River Walk bustled with visitors this time of year. The congestion funneled into the Wrong Way Diner —a regular hangout for locals—and the added business allowed Misty to store away the extra tips she earned. The tourist season enabled her to get by in the lean times.

"Hey. I made it." Carly had snuck up behind her. "I overslept." She smiled, tying her apron around her waist. Carly crashed at her boyfriend's three or four nights a week. When that happened, there was a fifty-fifty chance she'd make it to work on time. The predictable pattern didn't bother Misty...until today, when she was on the verge of exploding from the tension if she didn't tell Carly the news and soon.

Misty glanced over her shoulder. Carly's big blue eyes sparkled, pleading *don't be mad.* She shot Carly a *whatever* look. Leave it to Carly to show up at the tail end of the busiest hour.

"What's wrong?" Carly asked, sensing her attitude.

Misty blew out a long breath, feeling a touch lightheaded from the heat in the room. Face flushed, the need for fresh air became a necessity. She glanced around the room; the influx of customers had died down where she felt confident she could confide in her friend.

"Follow me." She took Carly by the elbow and dragged her over to a round table by the entrance so they wouldn't be overheard. A stale breeze drifted through the open front door and brushed her cheek, but it did little to relieve her heat distress. Misty pulled two towels out of her apron, tossed one to Carly, and began wiping the ketchup bottle.

Carly bent down and did the same to the maple syrup. "What's going on?" she whispered.

Misty stopped what she was doing and pinned Carly with a stare. "It turned blue." The scary words left her lips, and she waited for Carly's reaction.

Carly knitted her eyebrows. "What did?" She pretended to keep drying while she studied Misty's face.

"You know—the *test*," Misty hissed in a whisper so no one would overhear their conversation. She hoped Carly picked up on her meaning this time. They had talked about it two days ago.

"Oh...the *test*." Wide-eyed, Carly pushed for an answer. "What are you going to do?"

What could she do? She didn't have a lot of options. "What do you mean?"

"Are you going to tell him?"

Misty scoffed. It wasn't as though she could call up Beau Carson, rodeo star, and say, *"Hey, Beau, remember when we had a few cold beers several weeks back and landed in the sack after your big win? Well, I'm pregnant."* It was the one and only time they'd been together. They weren't dating or even friends. They'd just met at the bar and shared a few laughs.

Up until then, Misty had steered clear of experiences with men. Too many drinks later, they were at a hotel, and the night had haunted her ever since. She'd never done anything like it before. Shameful. It reminded her of her mother. Marla Summers had a reputation—a bad one. Misty shook her head.

Misty hadn't had any contact with her mother in over six years, not since she'd discovered Marla had fled the state with a new love interest, leaving Misty to deal with the overdue rent and fend for herself. She had no idea where they'd gone, and it didn't matter. She was tired of picking up the pieces of her mother's life and then rebuilding it when they'd moved from town to town.

Relationships left a bad taste in Misty's mouth, and she wouldn't repeat her mother's mistakes. She could return to her hometown of Crystal Cove, Florida, but would her grandmother speak to her after all that had happened?

Carly tilted her head to the side. "I think you should give him a call. After all, he might…"

"He might what?"

Carly was a hopeless romantic, but Misty wasn't interested in using a baby to snag a man. She had lived with the daily embarrassment of her mother's bizarre behavior growing up. Marla Summers believed a man would solve her problems when in fact it was the furthest thing from the truth. Reality had crystalized the night Misty bailed her mother out of jail…and once the charges were dropped, they'd skipped town together. In that moment of clarity, she'd realized everything she'd lost, including Bronson McCabe, her high school crush. From then on, her life had gone from bad to worse.

After a few tough years on the road, Misty had uncovered the truth. Her mother had fabricated a story to coerce Misty into fleeing Crystal Cove. Misty had left her only other family member: her grandmother. Believing her mother's lies, she hadn't spoken to her grandmother or been back to town since. Her shoulders slumped. She'd done everything in her power not to turn out like her mother. Being single and pregnant wasn't in her life plan. If she didn't break the cycle, she could wind up falling into the vicious trap of being alone with a child. She had to do something more for this baby. Her baby deserved what Misty had always longed for—a sense of family. Would her grandmother forgive her? She had to take a chance. She needed to give her child a life of love and stability, and there was only one place to do it—with her grandmother in Crystal Cove.

"This biscuit's hard as a rock." Bronson McCabe dropped it on the table to prove his point. It landed with a loud thud. His brothers Radford, Braxton, and Reese eyeballed it as it rolled to the floor with a thump. Another failed attempt. "Let's face it. None of us can prepare anything worth eating." The smell of burnt bacon still hung in the hazy air. Bronson glanced at the window where smoke from the smoldering cast-iron pan floated by. At least the grease fire was under control. He'd deal with the mess later. Right now, he was starving and so were his brothers.

Jim Crawley, the cook at the 4M Ranch, had eloped to

Las Vegas four days ago with a woman he'd met on the internet. That left Bronson and his three brothers to cook for themselves for the first time in their lives. The four grown men couldn't prepare a lick of food worth feeding to anything but the garbage disposal.

Their father had hired Jim twelve years ago to help out after their mother died. When Bronson's dad passed away a few years later, Jim had become the young ranchers' father figure. Now he was gone, and they were at a loss for a decent meal.

Radford frowned. "What if he never comes back?"

"Don't even say those words." Reese picked up his cowboy hat in disgust and placed it on his head. "I don't know about you three, but I'm going into town. I need something to eat…now." Radford and Braxton murmured their agreement as they made their way toward the door.

Bronson looked around the large country kitchen. All of the appliances were off, and there was no reason to sit there and starve. It wasn't a long ride into the center of Crystal Cove; he could keep his hunger at bay until then.

As the oldest of the McCabe brothers, Bronson had taken on the responsibility of managing the 4M Ranch and his brothers after their father died. Ranching was in his blood. He oversaw all six thousand acres with a thriving cattle and citrus business that supported a large majority of the tiny town. How hard could it be to figure this cooking stuff out? He'd work something out, and for their sake, it needed to be soon.

"I'll drive." Bronson followed his brothers outside to the truck. The four men climbed into the black Ford F-350. They needed a temporary cook while Jim was gone, but who?

The cool air blasted from the vents, and he hit the gas pedal a little harder than he'd intended, all too anxious to be on their way. He'd driven about six miles to the middle of town when he noticed a woman, with strawberry blonde hair and a suitcase, peeking in the windows of the old Summers place. The property sat on what used to be a pristine parcel of land on the corner of Galloping Hill Drive. His heart skipped a beat, could it be? *Nah.* He tamped down the urge to take a closer look. Maybe he should contact the sheriff. The woman looked like she needed some help. He slowed down, remembering the family that used to live there.

"What are you doing?" Braxton leaned over his older brother from the passenger seat and stared out the window. "Do you know her?"

He couldn't tell. Whoever she was she had her back facing them. Bronson thought something about her looked vaguely familiar. "I'm not sure." His stomach growled, and he decided not to give it a second thought. He let the truck begin to creep forward.

"You gonna stop and see if she needs any help?" Reese asked from the backseat.

Should he? It would be the gentlemanly thing to do. She might be lost. He watched her move around to the back of the house and almost caught a glimpse of her face. The hairs on the back of his neck began to rise. Could it be? Doubtful. Would Marla Summers show her face back here after all this time? The crazy woman was nothing but trouble. For years, he'd heard stories of how she'd broken her mother's heart.

Evelyn Summers had sat, day after day, on that front porch, pining away for the moment when her daughter and granddaughter would return. Now, it looked like Marla was back, and Evelyn wasn't here to see it.

He turned the truck around, pulled up to the house, and threw it in park.

"So close to food and yet so far," Radford joked.

"I hear ya," Reese added.

Bronson raised his eyes to the rearview mirror. "You two sound like you haven't eaten in days." Their mother used to comment how, with four sons, one of them was always starving. Reminded him of when they were kids. Their family laughed about how the four of them could eat them out of house and home and never gain an ounce. The hard work on the ranch kept the McCabe brothers muscular and lean.

"Want me to come?" Braxton asked.

"No, I'll be right back." He opened the truck door and stepped out. Evelyn Summers's house had seen better days. The weatherworn home sat in the center of the oversized property. The aged white paint, now grayed, peeled off in sheets from the wooden planks of the front porch. The lawn was sparse where grass had once grown. It looked more like a weed field. A rusted pail and watering can sat next to an empty flowerpot. Bronson remembered how charming the place used to be. The wrought-iron gate squealed as he pushed it open, and gravel crunched beneath his boots with each step up the driveway.

With his long stride, he arrived at the backyard quickly. The woman he was looking for had her face pressed against the glass window of the rear door. Now that he was closer, he realized this couldn't be Marla Summers. This woman was much younger than Evelyn's daughter would be. It couldn't be Misty either. His eyes feasted on the long, silky hair and sexy curves. No way was that sexy form the awkward lanky girl with fire-red hair he remembered from high school. The one who'd made a fool out of him when she'd stood him up at the Sadie Hawkins dance—and later skipped town with her mother.

He wet his lips. "Can I help you, miss?"

Startled, she jumped and spun around, her long hair fanning out around her face. "I was looking for my…"

She stopped mid-sentence, her gaze locked on his.

Bronson stiffened. Stunned, his eyes scanned Misty Summers from top to bottom.

Wow.

"Misty?"

It wasn't possible. Gone was the gawky girl from high school with sadness in her eyes. The bright red hair had transitioned to a sun-kissed strawberry blonde. And that gangly form now featured turquoise eyes, full ripe lips, and a pair of long legs that looked like they'd fit nicely around his hips. His heart skittered around in his chest. *Pull it together, man.* He reeled in his emotions.

Any daughter of Marla Summers, who looked like that, had to be trouble. More trouble than his ex-fiancée, Delilah. His momentary lapse of emotions now under control, he exhaled. "What brings you back here? It's been years."

She smiled. His breath crushed when she did.

Running her fingers through her long mane, she causally flipped it to the side. "Eight, actually. I came here to see my grandmother." Her hips swayed as she walked down the back steps toward him.

"I gathered that. But why now?" It seemed a bit odd she'd show up after all this time. Never once coming to visit. Not even—

"Do you know when she'll be back?"

He wasn't sure how to answer, then it hit him. She didn't know. He moved in closer, pushing his cowboy hat up to look deep into her eyes. Better to just come right out with it.

"I'm sorry to have to tell you this but...your grandmother passed away last year."

She'd missed her chance. Misty stifled the sob lodged in her throat. She turned around and faced the battered house she'd loved as a child. Tears welled in her eyes and began to trickle down her cheeks. Air squeezed in her lungs, and she released the breath she'd been holding. Her entire body shook with silent sobs. She wanted to know what happened but didn't have the strength to ask for details now.

Bronson came up behind her and rested his strong hands on her shoulders. "Why don't join us for breakfast, and we can talk." The compassion in his voice moved her. After all this time and the way she'd treated him the last time they'd seen each other, he was still a gentleman. *Us?* Join his wife and kids for breakfast? She wasn't sure.

"My brothers are starving and probably eating the leather

seats by now." He chuckled.

All of the McCabe brothers? She cringed. Heat rose to her face as she remember the way the group of four brothers had teased her when a ketchup bottle had exploded all over her blouse at school. That wimpy girl was gone, replaced by a strong, resourceful woman who had a baby to think about.

She turned and looked into his steel gray eyes framed by dark lashes. Warmth and tenderness filled them. She studied his chiseled features. He oozed masculinity blended with compassion. *How can I say no?* Drained from the bus trip and the news about her grandmother, she nodded.

Bronson walked over, pickup of her suitcase from the back porch, took her by the arm, and guided her around to front of the house. He motioned for his brother to open the front passenger door while he placed her suitcase in the back of the truck.

She tried to hide her face, embarrassed for them to see her raw emotion. She averted her gaze, avoiding eye contact with any of the McCabe brothers.

"You remember Misty Summers, guys, right?" Bronson asked. "She's a little shaken up. I had to tell her about Mrs. Summers."

All she could mumble was, "Hi."

Braxton moved out of the front passenger seat to allow Misty to get in, then he slid back in and shut the door.

A steady stream of tears dropped slowly into her lap. She couldn't tear her gaze from the sad-looking home as they drove off into town. *Good-bye, Grandmother.* If only she had returned to Crystal Cove sooner. They could have spent the quality time together Misty was looking for before she died. Now where would she go?

Grateful for the time alone, Misty roamed around the musty rooms of her grandmother's rundown house, numbed by the realization she had inherited the home and all of her grandmother's possessions. Her life had been a roller coaster of emotions over the past two weeks.

After they'd eaten breakfast a few days ago, Bronson and his brothers were kind enough to drive her over to the city hall. There, in the department of records, they had confirmed Evelyn Summers willed her house to Misty. She couldn't wrap her head around the series of events over the last few days. She'd discovered she was pregnant, quit her job to move back in with her grandmother only to find out she had died and willed her the house. Should she stay? What were her options with a baby on the way? For now, she would check into the Lakeside Inn located on the east side of town.

Over the years, Misty had lived in apartments or monthly rate hotels. Owning her own home had been a dream. Now it was a reality, and it gave her desperate situation an element of hope. Honored to have this opportunity, she cherished her grandmother's belongings and wanted to celebrate her life and memory. Somehow, she would find a way to make this house a home of her own in the quaint little town.

Everything inside and out now belonged to her, but the thought of digging through her grandmother's belongings made her uncomfortable, as if she were spying. It was strange to be here without her. Careful not to touch anything, she moved about the rooms, keeping her hands in her pockets. Every inch needed a deep cleaning to remove the dust and grime of a house sealed up for months. Once the power was turned on, she could begin to work on cleaning out the place. It was too hot to remain inside for any period of time without air conditioning or a fan running. She would have to extend her stay at the Lakeside Inn.

She hadn't known what to expect when she'd come back to town, but it sure hadn't been this turn of events. Misty took a deep breath and let the slight breeze cool her overheated skin as she walked out the back door and stood on the porch overlooking the backyard. She was still alone, no family to offer support or love, but maybe, in a way, her grandmother still watched out for her. She glanced back at the old home and smiled.

She needed to find a job before her funds ran out. What could she do? She walked down the steps and into the yard toward the detached two-car garage. She peered inside the windows. Her grandmother's Chevy was inside. Well, at least she had a car to use, even though odds were the battery was dead; it would take some money to have it serviced, money she didn't have. For now, she didn't mind walking wherever she needed to go in the small town.

She glanced around and saw another large object inside covered with a cloth. *What can it be?* She could wait until tomorrow to find out. It had been safely locked up for over six months—a day or two wasn't going to make a difference. Curiosity got the best of her, though. She unlocked the door and went inside. Lifting the edge of the cloth, she uncovered a large black cast-iron smoker. How strange. She'd heard stories about her grandmother's barbecue recipes but never realized it had been in the garage all these years. She dropped the cloth. The unbearable heat and a need for something cold to drink propelled her sense of urgency to get into some air conditioning—soon. One more quick run through the house before she left then to find a decent meal.

Inside, her shoes created an eerie echo of loneliness on the hardwood floors. Off the front entrance on the right was the dining room with a large antique chandelier hanging over the cherry table. White lace crocheted placemats and a table runner made the room look ready for a formal family dinner. She held back a sob. There wouldn't be any family dinners for the two of them.

On the left, in the living room was a sofa, two recliners, end tables, and a coffee table. Next to one of the recliners was her grandmother's crochet basket. Misty walked over and picked up the piece in progress, studying where her grandmother had left off. It had been years since she had practiced her stitches. She set the crochet down and walked into the kitchen. The ceramic bunny cookie jar rested on the counter in the exact same spot as it had years ago. How she coveted it as a child. Misty remembered carefully lifting the lid and reaching inside after school. It was always filled with some delicious treats her grandmother had made that day. How she wished when she was small the cookie jar could be hers, and now, her grandmother had willed it to her along with everything else.

She walked up the steps and into the master bedroom. On the long mahogany dresser was her grandmother's Bible. An oval frame held a picture with a Christmas holiday portrait of Misty with her mother smiling. Misty thought she'd been about five at the time. She remembered the day they went to the Sears portrait studio. Her grandmother had insisted they go; they had driven over an hour to the new mall to have this very picture taken. On the way there, her mother and grandmother had argued over something a five-year-old wouldn't understand. Later that night, her mother went out and didn't come back for several days. Misty and her grandmother went on as if nothing had happened.

Now, as an adult, Misty realized her grandmother had never let her worry. She'd pretended everything was fine, even though it wasn't. It was a way for them both to survive her mother's crazy abuse.

She was about to leave the room when she noticed a worn-out leather journal on her grandmother's nightstand. She walked over and picked it up. Flipping through the pages caused a few more tears to fall as she saw her grandmother's handwriting. She didn't want to leave the journal behind. She held it close to her chest as she walked down the stairs and out the front door.

The Lakeside Inn and Cafe wasn't far and something smelled delicious as she approached. The front porch was empty and the boards creaked as she walked along the long planks toward the front door. It may have been called a cafe on the outside but inside was a full bar along the wall and bunch of tables and booths to sit down. Two women sitting at a nearby table paused their conversation and studied her as she walked by. She had made it all the way to the takeout counter when she heard voice say, "Misty Summers, is that you?"

Turning to look at the semi-familiar face, she answered, "Yes."

Pale blue eyes sparkled with excitement. "Don't you

remember me? It's me, Darla." She approached, giggling, then threw her arms around Misty, giving her a gentle squeeze. "I can't believe it's you after all this time. I heard you were back." Darla Jenkins bubbled over with excitement. She hadn't changed much. Her long golden hair was pulled back on top with waist-length ringlets, and she wore the cutest little boots to match her pink sundress. Misty was conscious of her worn-out cutoff shorts and blouse.

"Really? I haven't been in town long." News traveled so fast here. How odd to meet Darla Jenkins and Bronson McCabe within her first few days in Crystal Cove. Darla and Misty were sort of friends. They weren't close, but the distance was Misty's fault. She could never be close with anyone for fear they might find out about her mother. In hindsight, she realized everyone already knew. She'd only been fooling herself. Even though Darla's family was one of the wealthiest in the county, they were always kind and down to earth. Darla had reached out to Misty growing up, including her in birthday parties and holiday events at her house. Misty had always appreciated being included.

Darla laughed. "Nothing stays a secret in Crystal Cove."

Misty flinched at the statement. Hopefully, her secret would—at least for the time being.

Darla released her hold. "So what gives? What are you doing back?"

It's really none of your business. "I decided to visit my grandmother." The words choked in her throat, and she turned away to hide her emotion. "I didn't know…"

"I'm so sorry." Linking her arm with Misty's, Darla pulled her over to the table where a younger woman sat waiting. "You remember my sister, Audrey, don't you?"

How could she forget Audrey? The girl had made a fool of herself chasing after Reese McCabe to the point of obsession back in middle school. Was she over her crush?

Thinking about Reese reminded Misty of Bronson. Was she over *her* crush? Kind of.

"She's married now and has a baby with Justin."

Question answered.

Darla went on. "She lives over in High Borough County."

"Nice to see you again." Audrey smiled.

"That's nice," Misty murmured, ignoring the details. She wanted to get a glass of ice water, and from the smells calling to her from the kitchen, taste whatever was being cooked. "I don't want to seem rude, but I really need something to drink and a bite to eat."

"Join us." Darla shoved her closer to the table and called to the kitchen for their waitress. "She'll be over in a minute."

"Thank you, but I really can't stay." She had planned to

order takeout and eat it back in her room. She needed to rest for a bit. After she'd eaten, the job hunt was on. Maybe she could get a position here at the Lakeside Inn. Most of her employment experience was in a diner or grill similar to this. Holding her grandmother's journal, she shifted uncomfortably from foot to foot.

"Are you sure?" Darla pouted in disappointment. "I thought we could catch up. Ya know, anything had to be more exciting than living in Crystal Cove."

Oh, her life had been exciting, but not in the way Darla meant. When you were down on your luck, the world could be a harsh, ugly place. Darla was fortunate enough to have been shielded by it because of her family's wealth. Misty wasn't bitter, but there were times when she'd wished for a different life. Still, she was grateful for all she had; she'd met others who were in a far worse situation.

Darla's pink lips frowned. "How long are you in town?"

"A while. Unless I can't find work," Misty said without thinking.

"Ohhhh." Darla held the syllable extra long. "What type of job are you looking for?"

Good question. At this point, she'd would take a job doing anything.

The waitress arrived, and Misty ordered a burger, fries,

and an ice water to go. The entire time Audrey never uttered a word, but sat there eating feverishly, her eyes fixed on her older sibling. Misty glanced at Darla's left hand. No wedding band.

Darla sat back down with her sister. "Well, I eat in town a few times a week. Maybe we can have lunch when you're all settled in."

Misty forced a smile. "Sounds great." She walked over to the counter, waited for her order, and paid her bill. On the way out of the cafe, she smiled at Darla and her sister.

She had a ton of unanswered questions where Darla Jenkins was concerned but she was too worn out to think about them now. She had so much to do now that she was home, and finding employment was on the top of that list.

Back in her room at the Inn, Misty relaxed and flipped the pages of her grandmother's journal. Oddly enough, it wasn't from recent years. It detailed the years when her mother was a child and her grandmother had entered the state fair. Recipes and itemized accounts of how she'd scored in each of the contests filled the inside. Misty engrossed herself in the notations off to the side. Hungry, she ate her burger. There was a recipe for barbecue sauce that made her mouth water. Boy, she'd love to dip her french fries in it. She realized the smoker in the garage was the very smoker her grandmother had described in the journal and had used to prepare her barbecued pulled pork, ribs, and brisket. It gave her an idea, and if it worked, some of her troubles may be over.

The chestnut mare steadied her footing on the rocky trail. Bronson eased her forward as he circled the perimeter of the 4M Ranch on horseback. It took hours to survey their property, but Bronson didn't mind. Riding the range for hours beat the alternative of trying to prepare a meal they could all enjoy. Sandwiches and Jiffy cornbread mix were becoming their steady diet, and the four brothers took turns making it. If they didn't find a replacement cook soon, they'd have to call off their workers' family appreciation picnic. For as far back as he could remember, the 4M Ranch had held their annual cookout, and he'd be damned if Jim's untimely marriage was going to ruin it. Bronson signaled the mare to pick up her speed. He needed to go back into town and put up a notice they were looking for a replacement for Jim, even if only temporarily. Until they heard back from him, he refused to believe the man had left their family for good.

Bronson stopped at a nearby pond so his mare could get a drink of water. The intense heat made it difficult to stay in the saddle, but clouds forming overheard forewarned of a storm on its way. He rode back toward the house, jumped down from the saddle, and handed the mare off to one of the ranch hands to be cooled down and groomed.

Over the past two days, he'd thought of Misty often. He wondered if she'd even remained in town. He was about to go find out when Radford stepped out onto the front porch.

Frowning, Radford shook his head. "Jim called. He won't be back for at least a month."

Bronson's stomach dropped. That settled it. They needed a temporary cook now and one who could cater the picnic, but in the small town of Crystal Cove, who could they hire? There weren't a lot of options. How dare Jim run off at time like this? Bronson refused to let down the families who worked so hard for 4M Ranch. This wasn't a regular old picnic; this was their chance to give back, and the McCabe family gave out amazing gifts to each and every family that day.

Radford reasoned, "We definitely need a replacement."

"I was about to go into town and begin our search. Wanna join me?"

"No thanks. Too many things to be done around here."

Radford always kept busy, checking on all of the livestock on their ranch property. The ranch had cattle, horses, chickens, and pigs. And great working dogs who were really more like babies than farm animals. Radford was a hands-on man and labored alongside the rest of the workers. Mending fences, feeding livestock, whatever needed to be done, he was right in the middle of it along with Bronson. Braxton and Reese took a different approach when they could.

"I might be a while. Call me if you need anything while I'm out." He made his way over to his truck and got in. "Don't worry. I'll pick up dinner in town."

Radford chuckled. "Thanks. I'm off cornbread duty tonight."

Bronson intended to cancel rock hard cornbread indefinitely. "Yup. A hot decent meal. No sandwiches. I'll be picking up a few casseroles from the Lakeside."

"They don't have casseroles, do they?"

"No. This is something new. I called to place an order, and she offered me some family-style dishes." He started up the truck and put down the window. "All I know is it's gotta be better than what we've been making."

Grinning, Radford fired back, "You know it."

When Radford laughed, he looked exactly like their father. Sandy brown hair and blue eyes, and that broad smile. Bronson didn't look anything like him; he favored their mother. Steel gray eyes and dark hair. Barbara McCabe was the town's beauty, and their father Roy worshiped her. She was the heart and soul of their family, and when she died, he lost it.

Reflecting on the past few days, Bronson focused his thoughts on his mission: hiring a cook. Why did something so simple seem so daunting? Bronson didn't like change. Maybe that was it. Jim had been there for years, and he would be coming back, right? The man deserved a life and some happiness. Did Jim know what he was really getting into? The entire situation opened the old wound of Delilah. Any talk of marriage had that effect on him. Delilah Pierce had made a fool of Bronson in front of the entire town. The humiliation was in the past, but the wound was raw and it stung nonetheless. He didn't know what hurt more—being left for another man or the embarrassment that he was too blind to see the deception. Even after all this time, he was undecided. He ground his teeth, letting his temper get the best of him. He flipped the air conditioner on high and accelerated to let off some steam. Anxious to have a talk with Arlene Hendricks, the owner of the Lakeside Inn and Cafe and one of the biggest gossips in Florida.

The Hendricks family had opened the diner the year Crystal Cove was established. The business had been passed down through the generations, and now it was Arlene's turn. She'd never been married, too afraid a man would take her money she said. So at sixty-three, she had a long-term boyfriend who helped out in the kitchen.

Bronson arrived at the restaurant a few minutes later and

killed the engine. The delicious aroma of smoky barbecue hit him when he opened his door. It smelled so good he wanted to taste the air. Walking over the threshold, he noticed several of the ranch hands sitting at tables about the room. He nodded greetings to several families. Arlene was standing behind the cash register. She looked up over a pair of reading glasses and smiled. Her pixie-cut red hair looked frazzled, and her chocolate brown T-shirt with the Lakeside Inn and Cafe written in yellow across the front was stained.

"Long day?" he questioned.

"Isn't it always?" she replied with sarcasm. For a short, stocky older woman, she as tough as nails, rough around the edges, and difficult to get close to. Bronson was used to her gruff demeanor. "I have your order ready. What are you boys going to do without Jim?" She called from the back while she retrieved the food.

"We have to hire a temporary cook." He half wanted to ask her if she could fill in, but decided to ask if she could recommend someone instead. "You don't know of anyone who could fill in, do you?"

"Can't say that I do. I can have the cook make you boys a tray of biscuits and some dinners, but I have a business to run and I can't lose my chef."

Well, she wasn't going to offer to help. "Thank you, Arlene. If you hear of anyone looking for work, let me know."

"Will do." She handed him the bags.

Bronson tossed several twenties on the counter. "Keep the change." He smiled—his visit now complete. He raised the bags, inhaling in the delicious aroma. "Something new?" he asked.

"Sure is. Let me know what you boys think of it." Arlene grinned with her yellowed smoker's smile.

He turned around and bumped right into Misty.

"Sorry. Excuse me," he stammered, juggling the bags so they didn't hit the floor.

"Sorry." She peered up, and brilliant white teeth smiled back at him.

Misty looked amazing in what seemed to be her house-cleaning clothes. Cutoff shorts and a scoop neck pink T-shirt covered in burgundy splatters—some women would look a mess, but to a man who was hungry she looked down right delicious. Her long hair was piled loosely on the top of her head. He wanted to release the shiny golden-red tendrils and run his fingers through them. He had been in a hurry, but now wanted to stop and make a little conversation.

"Are you getting settled in?" Would she be staying in town or cleaning up the house and listing it for sale? It could take a while. It wasn't as though a steady stream of people wanted to move to Crystal Cove.

"I am. There's so much to be done." She put her hands on the side of her face and shook her head in frustration. Long, thick brown lashes framed her cornflower blue eyes. He held her gaze.

Automatically, he offered, "I can swing by and give you a hand sometime."

Hope illuminated her face. "I'll take all the help I can get." Her full, ripe lips slipped into a smile. He pondered what they might taste like. Licking his lips in anticipation, he stepped closer.

"You'd be a fool not to," Arlene chimed in, adding her two cents. He'd forgotten she was behind him, examining the entire exchange under a microscope. Bronson turned, giving Arlene a "thank you, mind your own business" look.

"It's a bit overwhelming. The house needs a lot of repairs." Misty sounded dejected. "I won't be able to pay much for your trouble."

"There's no need." He didn't know why he'd started this conversation in the first place. His brain screamed *she's Marla Summers's daughter—run—steer clear.* "Have a good evening."

"You too," she mumbled.

He gave her a nod and breathed a sigh of relief once he'd

made it out the door. *Damn.*

Misty watched Bronson exit. *Well, he left in a hurry.* What did she expect? Bronson was a gentleman. He and the McCabe brothers might have helped her out the first day she'd arrived in town, but she shouldn't read anything more into it. A man like Bronson would look for a woman who could offer him something more. Not someone pregnant and with her family background. In the past, Bronson and his brothers had been known for helping out families in need in the community. The polite gesture lifted her spirits but not her hopes. Misty understood how he might feel after she'd stood him up at the Sadie Hawkins dance thanks to her mother's arrest that night.

She shrugged and faced Arlene. "How is the food selling?"

When Misty had approached Arlene for some type of employment, Arlene had explained her budget was way too tight. Being resourceful from years on the street, Misty had devised another plan, but she would need Arlene's help. She could prepare specialty dishes for Arlene to sell, and they would split the profits. Using her grandmother's barbecue recipe and the old smoker she'd discovered in the garage, Misty had been cooking all day. She'd tweaked the recipes to add a hint more heat, a personal preference, and smoked ribs, beef brisket, barbecued pulled pork, and barbecued chickens for sale. The regulars who dined at the Lakeside Inn and Cafe loved the new flavors of Misty's seasoning rub and her secret barbecue sauce. Several customers asked if she could bottle it for them. That sparked a new idea as dollar signs flashed into her mind.

"It's all gone. Bronson left with the last of it," Arlene said with a hint of satisfaction.

"Really?" Thrilled they'd sold out of everything. Misty calculated the profits in her head. If Arlene was agreeable, this could turn out to be a way for her to survive until she could find some steady employment.

"I can't say I'm surprised. This is a barbecue-loving town. Hell, Florida is a barbecue-loving state for that matter. You should think about entering your food in the state fair." Arlene pulled Misty closer and leaned on the counter. "I think you could win the grand prize of ten thousand dollars."

"Ten thousand dollars!" Misty exclaimed. With the prize money, she could repair her home and buy everything she needed for her baby.

Arlene brought her finger to her lips. "Shhh. Your

grandmother came close so many times and never won—that's another story—but you've done something special to this recipe. Your sauce is different. It's filled with love and hope, and downright delicious too." She leaned in even closer. "Keep it a secret until you decide to enter. News travels fast and wide in the county."

"I did put my own twist on her recipe." She'd added a few more spices and some extra heat to the sauce. For the pulled pork, she'd made a spiced pineapple chunk sauce with a touch of cayenne pepper and brown sugar. A concoction she was craving today. Misty had hoped the sweet, hot, and spicy flavor would be a favorite among the cafe clients. It tasted delicious to her. "Do you think I really have a shot at it?"

"I sure do." Arlene moved from behind the counter. "Wait here. I'll be right back." She winked and left through a small door to the side of the register marked office and returned a few seconds later, holding a piece of paper. "Here." Arlene shoved the paper into Misty's hand. She shifted her eyes around the room. "I think you've got a chance to win."

Misty read the bold print on the paper Arlene handed her. It was the entry form with the list of rules concerning the famous barbecue event held at the state fair. "Thank you. I'll definitely look into it." With a list of stipulations a mile long, she decided to read it later.

"If you have any questions, don't hesitate to call or come

by. I'll do the best I can to give you the answers." The older, petite woman tapped her pencil on the counter. "Now, how about we talk about your next batch of delicious food." Arlene gave Misty a warm smile.

"Arlene, I want to thank you again for giving me a chance. I can't believe the food sold out so quickly." Her heart fluttered with excitement. This was the opportunity she was looking for. If she could sell twice as much in a month as she had today, then with her portion of the money, she might be able to get the car repairs started. She had begun to look for a doctor in the next town over. Now that her suspicion had been confirmed, she needed prenatal care. Riding the bus to her OBGYN would take over an hour with all the stops. She was bound to get queasy in the heat. Worried she wouldn't be accepted if anyone found out about the baby, she had to come up with a way to keep it secret as long as possible.

"No thank-you is necessary. This has been a nice change. After fifty years working here, this added a spark to the old menu." She pulled out a cigarette from a pack hidden under the counter, and stuck it behind her ear. "Can't seem to quit, but I'm still trying." Arlene shrugged. "Watch the front for me while I go out back for a minute."

"Sure, no problem." She didn't mind, there wasn't much for her to do alone back at the house. She'd officially moved into her grandmother's house three days ago. She made a mental list of repairs, prioritizing them according to necessity. As the money came in, she could assign certain areas of the home to be mended. The roof was her biggest expense, but there were plumbing issues and the screened porch. She also wanted to make the home more her own by painting the walls to spruce up the place or adding a few personal touches. She couldn't wait to decorate the nursery, but she had time—seven and a half months to be exact.

By the time she delivered this baby, everything would be in place. She had no choice. This small, precious life depended on her, and she wasn't about to let her baby down. Not the way her own mother had let her down. This baby would grow up in a loving home. *But without a grandmother.* An ache pained her heart. If only her grandmother had lived. Misty knew for a fact she would never see her mother again. Not that she wanted to. The day her mother ditched her was the day Misty buried her mother. It had lifted the huge emotional burden she had been carrying. Years of trying to cover up for her mother's actions or deflecting the malicious comments from an intoxicated belligerent woman had taken their toll. Afterward it was so freeing to only have to worry about herself. Now she'd have a baby to consider, but that was different.

Tears began to form and threatened to fall. *Damn hormones.* She blinked and let the blurry mess trickle down her cheeks. She reached for a paper napkin to dab her face when Darla walked in. Averting her gaze to the sheet on the fair entry requirements helped to regain her composure.

Darla dashed over to the counter where Misty sat trying to salvage her dignity. The woman looked like she was dressed out of a magazine, perfectly tailored in a lace-trimmed halter dress. Misty self-consciously adjusted her clothing. But her worn out, barbecue-sauce-splatted work clothes couldn't compare to Darla's crisp, clean look, with not a hair out of place.

"Hey, Darla. How can I help you?" Pushing her situation out of her mind, she forced a stale smile.

"Are you all right?" Darla questioned. She knitted her eyebrows. A lopsided grin graced her lips. "I'm here if you need to talk."

Misty wasn't about to discuss the baby with anyone, at least not yet. "I'm fine. I have a speck of dust in my eye." She never did get used to being alone; it was difficult at times and this pregnancy made her more emotional than usual. She disliked when she showed any sign of weakness.

Darla sympathized. "I hate when that happens. At least you don't have mascara and eyeliner running down your face."

Who could afford it? Makeup was a luxury, and she didn't waste what little she had wearing it every day.

"What can I do for you?" Misty asked, getting to the point of their visit.

"Your barbecue—" Darla started but Misty held up her hand and interrupted her.

"I've sold out. I'm sorry. I can make you some tomorrow." Business had started off with a much bigger need than she'd anticipated. Distracted, she was anxious to read the instructions on how to enter the state fair. Darla paused, waiting. The response Misty had received from the customers gave her the encouragement to dream big. Tomorrow she would bring in oversized muffins, cakes, and fresh pastries.

Darla laughed. "Thank you, that would be wonderful, but that's not what I was going to ask." She had a strange look of excitement on her face. Confused, Misty couldn't figure out what Darla wanted. Usually she could read people, a skill she'd developed from observing situations when in survival mode. Misty had no clue what Darla was up to.

"I had your barbecue pork sandwich this afternoon. It was fantastic. When do you want to have lunch this week?"

Could it be that simple? Darla wanted lunch? Doubtful. "Let me check my schedule." Supplying the Lakeside Inn with meals would filled up her time.

"Sure. Here's my cell number." Darla shoved a small piece of paper in front of Misty.

Arlene returned from smoking her cigarette. "That was fast," Misty commented.

"It's too hot to sit out there and enjoy my smoke." Arlene looked wilted from the heat. She walked around the counter, taking her post behind the cash register. "Thank you for holding down the fort." The musty smell of cigarettes and sweat made Misty want to gag. She moved out of the way and smiled. "It was a piece of cake."

"Why don't you let me know what your menu is going to be." She turned to Darla. "How can I help you?"

Darla ignored Arlene and asked Misty, "Speaking of cake —can you bake too?"

"Uh, um, yes. As a matter of fact, tomorrow I'm going to bake a few cakes and pastries to have available." She hoped she had the ingredients for what she needed at the house already.

She decided to go back home and get some rest. Tomorrow would be another busy day. She picked up the sheet of paper Arlene had given her. Folding it, she shoved it in the back pocket of her shorts. Forgetting Darla, she headed out the door and returned her concentration to winning the prize money. *Ten thousand dollars.* What a difference that kind of money could make in her life. She left the Lakeside Inn and began the brief walk home. If she was going to be a serious contender at the state fair, there was a lot of planning to do.

When she reached the front stoop, she unlocked the door and pushed it opened. The smoky scent still hung in the air inside, even worse it clung to her hair and clothing. A cool shower to relieve her overheated body seemed to be in order after a long day outside in the Florida heat. Standing next to the smoker had taken its toll on her physically. She pulled the folded paper out of her rear pocket, eager to devise a winning strategy. The requirements seemed doable but a little more than she'd expected. As she scanned farther down the page, a huge obstacle halted her.

How in the world would she pull this off? In order to be considered, all entrants must supply enough food samples for the hungry fairgoers. Her hopes dwindled. She withered with despair. No. She shook her head. The prize money was her only chance for survival…to be independent. She mustn't allow one hiccup to destroy her plans.

She mulled over different options as she climbed the stairs on her way to the shower. By the time she reached the top step, the perfect solution popped into her head. There was only one way she could enter and win, but she must have the help of Bronson McCabe.

Debra Fisk

3

"I see what you mean." Bronson had been called out into the field by one of the younger ranch hands to assess the situation. *Why the heck aren't my brothers around to take care of this?*

"Sorry. I tried to contact Radford before I called you all the way out here, but I didn't know what else to do." New to the ranch, Jessie, the inexperienced cowboy wore a perplexed expression. Bronson would use this as a teaching moment for the youth, but why the hell wasn't one of his brothers or a seasoned ranch hand out here with him?

Having Lady, his border collie, round up the cattle should have made the chore much easier, but today, Bronson had had no such luck. Lady knew her duty and was the best herder the ranch had, but she was agitated because she was going have pups soon. Bronson had started to suspect it last week, except her pregnancy shouldn't have been possible. The shelter they'd adopted her from said she'd been spayed. He frowned at the mix-up. Lady stared down the herd, grouping them together, while King, their Welsh corgi, nipped at the livestock's hooves to move them toward cooler areas under the trees and into the ponds away from the direct sunlight.

The early morning heat was intense already. Both Lady and King were having a difficult time pushing the cattle out from under a small cluster of trees on the terrain and directing them to the pond where huge thick oak trees hugged the shoreline, providing ample shade.

One of the many challenges of being a rancher was keeping your cows cool in the extreme Florida summer. Something had spooked them from the pond, and after hearing about the cattle they'd treated for venomous snake bites this morning, Bronson knew what it was. A large family of pit vipers must have settled into or around the pond. It wouldn't be the first time he and his brothers had run into this problem. What he needed was a few of the ranch hands with a couple of catch poles to pull them out of the water and place traps to lure the ones on land.

Once collected, they'd deliver them to the serpentarium that supplied universities and a number of pharmaceutical companies with snake venom for research and anti-venom production for the entire country. Most people wouldn't think twice about shooting the snakes on the spot; however, living so far from a hospital made him respect nature all the more. He had a responsibility to do his share to preserve the environment. They also kept a supply of anti-venom on hand at the ranch.

His phone buzzed, and he glanced down at the screen. Reese. His mood soured. Where the hell had his brother been? He'd tried calling him for the past hour with no response.

"Where the heck are you?" Reese asked when Bronson connected the call.

"Me? I've been calling you for over an hour. I'm doing your job," Bronson answered, his voice tight. "Why? What's wrong?"

"There's someone here to see you at the house. Want me to send her out there or are you going to come back here?"

"Her?" *Who the heck wanted to see me?*

"Misty," Reese said with a sweetened tone. "Said she *needs* to talk to you."

It didn't make any sense. Why would Misty drive all the way out here to talk to him? He had his hands full today. The herd, vipers, and at some point, he must make time to go back into town to find Jim's replacement or at the very least pick up a few more meals from the Lakeside Inn.

He glanced at the wide-eyed cowboy next to him then spoke to Reese. "Drive out here to big oak pond and take over for me. I'm on my way."

Bronson didn't care what she wanted; the answer was *no.* He'd better keep his distance. If it was about the repairs, he'd given that careful thought and decided he'd send someone out to her house—no problem. That must be why she was here.

He filled Jessie in on the problem with the pond and told him to wait on Reese, then he walked over and got in the truck to head back to the main house. When he pulled up, he saw a vehicle parked out front. He recognized Arlene's car. She must have been kind enough to loan it to Misty. Interesting. If Arlene had shown random acts of kindness before, he'd never been witness to it. This was a first.

He parked his truck and headed toward the house. On the way, he lifted his hat off his head and wiped the sweat from his face with a cloth he kept in his back pocket. He placed his hat back on, opened the screen, and hurried inside the back door, eager to see why Misty had stopped by.

Misty and Reese sat at the kitchen table, drinking iced tea. Misty shifted her gaze to him with apprehensive eyes and bit her lower lip. She wore a weathered, denim sundress, but it was pressed, and her hair was pulled away from her face with long curls cascading down her back. Her hair looked shiny and soft. The reddish hue glowed around her face.

Seeing Bronson enter, Reese got up, turned to Misty, and said, "See you later." He placed his drink in the sink, then walked over to where Bronson stood.

Bronson wasted no time in filling Reese in. "Vipers are disrupting the cattle at the oak pond."

"I'm on it." Reese nodded then left the two of them alone. Bronson removed his hat and raked his fingers through his sweat-damp hair.

Getting right to the point, he asked, "You wanted to see me?"

She grabbed her glass of iced tea and sipped it through the bent straw. Her eyelashes fluttered nervously then she looked up, pushed back the chair, and stood. Taking a few steps forward, he looked down into the cornflower blue pools framed by dark brown lashes. Her lips tugged into a smile, the tip of her tongue peeked out and moistened them before she spoke.

Softly, she said, "I have a favor to ask."

Captivated by the vulnerability in her eyes, he listened, prepared to deflect any request she made. With his automatic response already rehearsed, he waited for her to continue. She shifted from one foot to the other, and he glanced down at her scuffed, short, brown boots—they had seen better days.

"What kind of favor?" he pressed.

She cleared her throat. "I cooked the barbecue Arlene served yesterday at the Lakeside Inn or, as Arlene likes to call it, Lakeside Cafe. I'm planning on entering the state fair this year." She paused and blew out a long breath.

Surprised, he said, "You cooked it? It was delicious. From what I tasted, I'd say you have a pretty good chance of winning then." The food had been amazing. The four of them had sat in this very kitchen last night and agreed it was the best barbecue they had eaten in years—maybe even ever. He and his brothers wondered why Arlene had never served it before. Now he knew.

Her expression lit up, and her smile stretched to show her perfect white teeth. "Thank you. It's the fair that I need the help with."

"I don't understand. How can I help?" He wasn't about to man a smoker if that was what she was thinking. Hell, none of them could, and he didn't have a cook to help her either.

"One of the rules of the fair states…when you enter the barbecue cook-off, you agree to provide food to the fairgoers. It's a lot of food. I was going to ask you if I can purchase what I need at a wholesale price…" Her voiced squeaked. Then she added, "And I'll need it on credit." Her smiled faltered, replaced by a troubled feature. "I can pay you back the money from my sales at the fair." She sounded confident, and it almost convinced him. Almost.

He'd like to help her out, but this was Marla Summers's daughter. The woman had lived a life of broken promises and lies. Positive Misty must have learned a scheme or two from her mother, he'd have to decline. After all, she'd never shown a hint of remorse for standing him up at the dance eight years ago. No, he should turn her down flat and stay away from her.

Right now, his day-to-day life ran smooth with the ranch and his brothers. Somehow, he had a feeling if he took the plunge and said yes, things would take a downward turn. Besides, what would his brothers say? He would never hear the end of it. It was bad enough he'd been the laughing stock back in school after the dance. For months, they'd teased him about how he'd been left waiting—jilted by Misty, a skinny, clumsy, and awkward girl—but the woman before him was none of those things —far from it. She was hot, sexy, and would use that to her advantage for sure.

Apprehensively, he said, "It seems like a lot of risk on my part. Plus, if it didn't work out, it would place you in a tight financial position." He rubbed his stubbled chin in thought. "I don't see any benefit on my part. I have everything to lose." It was true. If she didn't sell enough product at the fair, he would be the one out the money. He also knew if she was unable to pay him back after the contest, he wasn't about to pressure her for the funds.

From what he could tell, she didn't have much except for the worn out things her grandmother left her in the will.

"I understand your hesitation and why you believe it's too much of a risk." She leaned in closer, and the scent of something sweet like vanilla blended with lemons tickled crosses his senses. It smelled good—warm—nice. "You said yourself I have a pretty good chance at winning," she added.

He did say that and he meant it. Thinking about the mouthwatering feast they'd had last night and how he would enjoy meals like that every night gave him an idea.

"I'll make you a deal. I'll agree to supplying you with the meat you need for the fair, and I'll supply it to you on credit, but you have to agree to do something for me." He smiled. If she was willing, his problem was solved.

She stopped smiling and her mouth slumped into a frown. "What did you have in mind?"

It was a perfect solution to their problem. His brothers couldn't fault him for this. "Jim, our longtime cook, ran off to get married, and he's going to be gone a few more weeks. My deal is this, you agree to cook the food for our workers' appreciation picnic, and I'll supply you with everything you need for the fair. After what I tasted last night—with your skills and talent it's bound to be a success."

She remained silent, pressed her lips together in

consideration. With a shrug, she said, "Sure, no problem. It'll be a good practice run for the fair."

As an afterthought, he added, "Oh and one more thing. We are in desperate need of a cook until he gets back. Would you be interested in a job—you know, cooking for us?" Bronson wasn't opposed to begging if it came to it. "Ranch work is hard physical labor. We need three decent meals a day. None of us can make something edible." The bowls of cereal were lacking the daily substance the men needed.

Misty stared at Bronson—arms folded across his broad chest, collar-length sandy brown hair and steel gray eyes hypnotized her to nod her agreement. An inner sigh touched her heart. She watched his mouth move when he spoke. He explained the temporary desertion of Jim, and the situation he and his brothers faced. She wondered if it was a dream. She needed a job and his help. Normally, she didn't like to make deals, but in this case, she didn't have a choice, and besides, it seemed like it would be fun to cook for the picnic. As for taking over for Jim, their cook, she wanted to jump up and down screaming yes. This was exactly what she needed.

Instead, she smiled and said, "Sure, no problem."

Bronson wrapped his arms around her and gave a tight squeeze. "You can start today. Right now as a matter of fact." He released her, and she thought the air would never return to her lungs. The strength of his tight grip sent heat to her cheeks. She glanced up, hoping he didn't notice the effect he had on her.

"Arlene's probably wondering where I am with her car." She'd borrowed it at dawn, and it had taken longer than she had expected to run a few errands. She hoped her only friend in Crystal Cove wasn't too upset. Arlene had been kind and treated her with respect when she'd first arrived. She'd been friends with Misty's grandmother for years before her death. Misty didn't want Arlene to feel she was taking advantage of her generosity.

Earlier, she had driven over to see a doctor in the next town. He'd confirmed her pregnancy, drawn blood, and ordered her to take prenatal vitamins. Then he'd announced her due date was March 8. From that point on, it all seemed so very real. Before the spring, she would be a mother. What would Bronson and Arlene think about her then? She shoved those unproductive thoughts into a dark corner in her mind. She'd cope with the situation later.

"Why don't you return the car, and I'll follow you back into town. After we shop and pick up the supplies you'll need, I can drive you back here." Bronson seemed to have it all planned out. "Then you can use one of the trucks we own to drive back and forth then you won't need to borrow Arlene's car."

"Are you sure?" Her pulsed danced erratically. Being close to Bronson all day would test her sense of self-control. Would she pass or fail?

He grinned. "Absolutely." He stepped a bit closer and her temperature rose, heat flushed her cheeks. Bronson's coloring remained the same; by the looks of things, she was the only one affected. *Damn.* She wasn't over her crush. *Why aren't any of the McCabe brothers married?* The hottest most eligible men in a two-hundred-mile radius and they all remained single. There had to be a reason—didn't there?

"Ready?" he asked. She snapped out of her daydreaming, and her body's response cooled. His casual mannerisms reminded her that men like Bronson didn't fall for women with her family history.

She cleared her throat. "Yes.

"Then let's get to it." He motioned toward the back door.

She glanced around the large kitchen as she left the room. He was fortunate to grow up in a traditional family, with a mother and a father who loved each other and their children. When Misty was a child, she often imagined what it might be like to have known her father. What was he like? How did her mother meet him? Even a more disturbing thought, did her mother even know who he was? If she did, she'd never mentioned it, and her grandmother had remained silent on the subject.

On occasion, she'd try to pry the information out of her mother one way or another, but she'd only given vague answers and glossed over any details. Growing up without a father figure made her feel like an outcast in a place where everyone was neighborly and the traditional families outnumbered the broken homes. She'd mourned the childhood she'd never had. How she had longed to participate in the father-daughter dance like the other girls had. Her heart clenched.

Things would be different for her baby. Somehow she would raise her child alone. The two of them would be a real family together—supportive, caring, loyal. Her heart swelled with the endless love she already had for this child. Marla had grown up fatherless, but that was where the similarities between her and her mother had ended.

Misty's grandparents had married young. When her grandmother discovered she was pregnant, her grandfather left Crystal Cove for a better job opportunity. He was gone only a month when he was killed in an oil rig accident off the coast. Her grief-stricken grandmother had received a modest settlement but not enough to raise little Marla. Somehow her grandmother got by. Misty didn't want to just get by; she wanted to support her child. That was why having a plan for a future was so important. She turned and looked at Bronson, so strong and proud. His family business thrived and he had his brothers to rely on. Misty only had herself.

Bronson stood, holding open the door. "After you." She glided out the door, down the steps, and over to Arlene's car. She looked back over her shoulder and caught Bronson watching her. Quickly, she turned away.

As she was getting in, he said, "I'll pick you up at the Lakeside Inn."

Lord, how was she going to survive being so close to the man and not make a fool of herself?

Bronson followed at a distance as Misty drove Arlene's car back to the cafe. He wondered what her life had been like after she had left Crystal Cove. Where had she been living all this time? Up until now, he hadn't really thought to ask. He'd been too self-absorbed with Jim's absence to think straight. The cook's surprise marriage had stirred up old painful emotions Bronson had buried down deep. Misty's unexpected return rattled another set of feelings he'd rather avoid.

When he was separated from Misty, like now, his

common sense warned him to proceed with caution, but when they stood in the same room, any skepticism he had about her disappeared. Because of Delilah's deception, Bronson considered himself a lousy judge of women. He also believed women with true values, like his mother, were a thing of the past. In his opinion, it was rare these days to find a woman who wasn't materialistic or harboring a hidden agenda.

He absorbed the beauty of the scenic drive. It gave him a chance to clear his head and rehash the past—sorting out the details of his life. The 4M Ranch thrived now more than ever before, and the McCabe men were financially taken care of, yet none of them could find a woman to date who wasn't trying to rush them down the aisle. What was wrong with getting to know each other before hitting the sack? In part, they were the most eligible bachelors in the county, which made it difficult to find a woman. Most women were interested in his position in society; he wanted a woman who was interested in him and a life on the ranch—plain and simple. He hadn't met a woman yet who met his qualifications. Was he asking too much?

He reexamined the events that lead to him fabricate this deal. What was he thinking? Could Misty be trusted not to run off again? Doubtful. Memories of his disastrous engagement to Delilah floated to the surface. She'd left with a rodeo star—a longtime friend no less—for the glitz and glamour a rancher's lifestyle didn't offer. Twice he'd been embarrassed in front of the town. By Delilah and, years past, as a youth by Misty. He'd accepted her offer to go to the Sadie Hawkins dance out of sympathy really, and he'd admired her courage to even ask. Saying yes was a way to show her how sorry he was for the way he and his brothers had teased her.

At the time, he hadn't been interested in dating, with a ranch to manage and his brothers to look out for. They'd lost both of their parents before they'd graduated high school, and the sole weight of responsibility of the ranch and his brothers had landed on Bronson's shoulders. Dealing with that type of loss made a young man grow up fast. Which brought his mind back to Misty. Where was her mother? Was she still alive?

He pulled in front of the Lakeside Inn, suspending that thought, silenced the engine, and flung open the door. The smell of a greasy grill hung in the sizzling hot air. He looked over his shoulder at the center of town. The same seven buildings had lined the horseshoe-shaped street since before he was born, the businesses passing down from generation to generation.

The Jenkins family owned and operated the grocery store, a large brick structure that stood at the center of the block. The 4M Ranch supplied them with meat and poultry. Off to the left, was the white church with a towering steeple, which backed up to a lush open field. To the right of the church were two smaller flattop buildings—the barbershop and the hair salon. There was two-story town hall, which housed the mayor's office, sheriff's department, and official records bureau. The Lakeside Inn behind him, of course, and on the opposite side of the street was the general store, which sold everything from guns and bait and tackle, to clothing, fabric, and feed. All the basics a person needed in life were supplied right here.

He shut the door just as Misty emerged from the cafe. She looked adorable in her faded blue, denim sundress— feminine—sexy. As she drew closer, he inhaled the sweet scent of vanilla, savoring the hint of lemon she wore. He loved anything citrus. She smelled delicious, fresh and clean, not full of sweat like him. Her smile did something to his insides, and he shook it off to break the trance he'd fallen into. He dipped his head lower to shield his eyes from the afternoon sun.

Then he motioned with his head in the direction of the grocers. "They should have everything you need at Jenkins." If not, they could drive to the next town, but that would take a while.

"I have to admit, I'm kind of excited and a little nervous about the idea." She looked up at him as they fell into step side by side. Her large blue eyes sparkled with excitement. She glowed as if something thrilling was about to happen.

"Don't be. You'll do just fine." He didn't know what made him say that, but he felt deep inside it would be.

She had a knack for cooking, and his brothers had a knack for eating.

They moved in perfect unison as they approached the front entrance, both reaching for a shopping cart at the same time. Their hands touched, sending a jolt throughout his body. It had been a long time since he'd been with a woman—too long—and the effects had obviously caused him to be extra sensitive to her nearness. She pulled the cart toward her but he easily maneuvered it away. He didn't mind steering it up and down the aisles. She tilted her head, giving him a sideways glance, and the crooked smile revealed a tiny dimple in her cheek. He didn't remember seeing her smile quite like that before and he liked it.

She laughed. "I can handle it. I don't mind." She shifted her gaze forward to hide her face as she blushed a deeper shade of pink. That puzzled him. Could she tell he was attracted to her? He thought he'd masked his feelings much better than that.

They stepped through the automatic doors and a blast of cold air him in the face. His overheated body welcomed the crisp breeze, thankful for the relief from the temperatures outside. Misty shivered in her sleeveless dress.

"I have a small blanket in the cab of the truck. I'll be right back." He turned to leave, and she placed her hand on his arm to stop him. He look down where she held his forearm; his skin tingled with excitement.

"I'm fine. I'll be all right." The twinkle in her eye held his gaze, willing him to stay, so he did. He wrestled to free himself from their trance.

"If you change your mind, it will only take me a minute." Surely she needed that blanket, and he needed to take a few steps back or he would be falling for her and that was impossible. His life couldn't support a relationship now —not ever.

"I want to focus on the meals you and your brothers like and what I will need for the family appreciation picnic." She began to ask him questions, and he fired off answers about what they liked to eat after a long hard day working on the ranch. She placed items in the cart like a machine, so fast it was filled to the brim.

"Wait here." He wheeled it up to the front and placed it by the cashier. "I'm taking all of this and about to fill another one," he said to the young girl chewing gum and filing her nails out of boredom.

"Sure, no problem," she answered through the bubble she blew that hid her face.

He returned to where he'd left Misty, and she was grinning ear to ear, her face covered with amusement.

"Something comical?" Puzzled, he wondered why she was laughing at him. He was curious why she found grocery shopping, which he despised, funny.

"Well, kinda. I've never filled a basket, let alone needed a second one." She giggled. "Most of the time what I'm buying I can carry out in one of those little arm baskets. This is fun."

"What about holiday meals with your mother?" She had to have shopped for more than an armful then? Misty's eyes dimmed, and he immediately regretted mentioning Marla Summers. He cursed silently under his breath.

"I haven't seen or spoken to her in years," she murmured and moved ahead of him down the aisle. "I doubt I will ever again." Her voice trailed off while she walked away searching the shelves to avoid looking directly at him. He yanked the cart with force and pushed it to the side.

He sped up to glide along her left side, offering his sympathy. "I'm sorry I mentioned it." He was, but at least now he knew she was all alone in this world, and that meant she needed his help all the more. Something niggled in the back of his mind. Why was she here? She'd come back for a reason. He was sure of it. But what? Trouble most likely. Jealous husband or ex-boyfriend—possibly worse. If she was a hint like her mother, there would be something for sure.

Misty tried to recover from the reference to her mother, an old wound that had never healed. How could it? The woman had abandoned her at an early age for yet another dysfunctional relationship destined to fail. Her self-worth immediately suffered whenever she thought back to the moment she'd woken up and realized she was all alone. Misty could never ever leave her baby. *The two of us will always be together.* She placed her hand over her stomach and sighed.

"Do you feel okay?"

Lost in thought, she jumped at the sound of Bronson's rich, soothing voice. Scrambling to collect her composure, she cleared her throat. "I'm fine." She had to be. There wasn't any room in her world for pity or regret. Her baby deserved a future filed with love—not that of an unwanted burden. Even though her life was lacking, she had so much to be thankful for compared to other young women in her situation. Moving from town to town, she had seen every imaginable situation of an unwed mother.

"I might as well tell you about it now. I'm sure you've figured out my mother wasn't much of a mother. She had —" Misty groped for the right word. "Issues." That was an understatement. "It's been over six years since we've spoken. She decided to leave in the middle of the night with her boyfriend at the time and the rent overdue." She blew out a long breath. "The worst part is…I believed her lies about my grandmother. And that kept me from speaking to her. Now she's gone, and I'll never have that chance to say I'm sorry." Her voice cracked as she strangled a sob in her throat. Tears pooled and threatened to spill over. She dabbed her eyes and tried to mask her pain by changing the subject. "How about a peach cobbler tonight for dessert?" She wanted to lighten the mood now that her emotions had gotten the best of her. She squirmed when Bronson looked moved by her confession and dodged around to the side of the cart, pretending to adjust the groceries. *Damn hormones.*

He paused in silence then said, "That sounds delicious."

What a gentleman. Her insides flopped like melted Jell-O. He knew how to make a girl feel cozy. *Don't get any ideas.* Bronson was off limits. Forget about the broad chest and strong arms. How would it look if she fell for him? Foolish. He was out of her league, even more so now that he knew the truth about her background. No, she was better off reining in her pregnancy hormones while she had her wits about her. Imagine when the word got out around town that she was pregnant? Tossing the nerve-racking thought into the back of her mind, she asked, "How about pot roast for tonight with mashed potatoes and biscuits—oh, and a crisp green salad."

"Sounds perfect, except you can forget the salad. We don't eat too much rabbit food." He chuckled. His happy smile washed away her sadness and her mood lifted.

Then with a stern hard look, she frowned and said, "I'm making salad, and you boys are going to eat it." Determined to serve a balanced healthy meal, she cocked her head and arched her eyebrow in a bold I-dare-you-to-mess-with-me move.

"Well—okay then." He grinned that fabulous grin. The one that made her insides quiver.

Oh, she was in deep—well over her head. This was trouble. The worst kind.

They finished up the shopping and made their way to the front. The young cashier flipped an annoyed glare at them as she tossed the magazine she was reading onto the pile next to her register, no doubt irritated she had to work for a change. In silence, she rang up the items then stabbed them with a frigid stare as they walked out the door. Misty struggled to contain her excitement. Never in her life had she imagined someone could spend that much on food. Sure, the picnic was a huge event, but the amount of groceries being allocated to the McCabe brothers fascinated her. Whenever she mentioned an ingredient or spice she could use, Bronson told her to get it or took it upon himself to toss it in the basket. It would take over an hour to put it all away; she was sure of it.

He turned on the air conditioning and told her to relax as he loaded up every inch of the truck. He finished, then opened the driver's door and slid in next to her. He reached in the back for a small towel and patted his face dry.

"I've lived here all my life. You'd think I'd get use to the heat." He sat and relaxed for a brief second then threw the truck into reverse and backed out to return to the 4M Ranch. "Do you need to stop by your house for anything?" he asked. His dampened shirt pressed against his hard muscular chest, and she wondered what it would be like to be pressed up against *him*.

Fanning her face. "No, thank you." She appreciated his concern but she had a lot of work to do. "We better get back. I plan to dive right in and get started, this way dinner will be ready by six." Then she added, "If that's all right."

"I'm looking forward to it." He winked with a crooked grin. "Jim might not have a job to come back to."

Worried, she assured him, "Oh no, I could never do that. I would never try to take away Jim's job. I couldn't live with myself." She would never deliberately calculate to remove Jim as the longtime cook for the 4M Ranch.

Just then Bronson's cell phone buzzed on the seat. Misty glanced at the screen to see the name *Braxton* lit up in bold print. Bronson fumbled for the cell phone as he drove. Finding it, he hit the accept button.

"Yeah." His eyebrows knit together as he listened to his brother on the other end then frowned. His nostrils flared and he seemed to get upset. "All right. I'm already on my way. I'll be home soon. Have you called the doc?" He paused to listen. "I see." He ended the call and tossed the phone back on the seat.

Agitated, Bronson pressed the gas pedal harder and they jolted forward. Concerned, Misty asked, "Everything okay?" She squirmed in her seat, uncomfortable at his mood change. The men who had dated her mother often angered easily, and she didn't want to witness an outburst here.

"Yes and no. Just everyday ranching life. Nothing is every easy, is it?" He shrugged then added, "The thing is —with my brothers—well—they look to me to solve everything since I'm the oldest. Most of the time they can take care of it themselves."

He seemed to be less agitated, and the knot that had formed in her stomach relaxed.

"I'm sure they can but would like to have their older brother's approval." She studied him as he drove. So confident and sure of himself; his brothers must feel inadequate. Bronson's example was a hard one to follow. He seemed to always know the right thing to do. For the other three McCabes, she surmised it was probably easier to ask Bronson rather than risk making a wrong decision. He'd shouldered the responsibility of raising his brothers and managing the ranch since his father's death. Life forced him to grow up in a hurry, but his brothers hadn't had to—not really, from what she understood.

Braxton was a smooth-talking gentleman—a real ladies' man, rumor had it. Radford was a bit of a hothead whose fiery temper got the best of him and created situations his brothers had to help him out of, and Reese—the intellectual—a laid-back observer who was indecisive. Seeing situations from both sides prevented him from making a decision, so he wound up messing around and goofing off.

"They don't need it. Not if they use their common sense." He gave her a look with raised eyebrows. Yup, just as she'd suspected, he wouldn't be too forgiving if a mistake was made. Her thoughts shifted to her situation. How would he view her pregnancy when he found out? How would he view her? She cringed at the thought, then buried it down deep inside.

"What's the doctor's name?" Not that she'd go to the only doctor in town, but she didn't want to see a friend of the McCabe family. She hadn't even bothered to look him up. Even though there was doctor-patient confidentiality, how would she explain the frequent visits? In a small town like this, it was only a matter of time until someone noticed she was going to the doctor a little too often.

"Harrison. Doc Harrison. He's new to the area."

Harrison. She made a mental note for when she bumped into him in town, and there was no doubt in her mind she would.

"He's meeting me out at the ranch. A bull clipped one of our new hires and flung him up against the fence." He paused and blew out a long breath. "Broke his leg for sure. Braxton's waiting for Doc Harrison to arrive." He looked over at her, and she could feel a sense of awkwardness come between them. "I'm sorry but I'm going to have to unload the truck and leave you to put everything away in the kitchen so I can head out to the accident."

Instinctively she reached over and touched his shoulder. "I understand. Don't worry about a thing. I can manage." She smiled to relieve him of any responsibility he might feel for her. She was used to managing so much more on her own. She swallowed the bitter pill of loneliness she tasted every time she thought of her life on the road. In a few months, everything would be different; she wouldn't be alone. The baby—her baby—would fill every minute of her life. Would Bronson still be in her life? She closed her eyes. That remained to be seen.

The back door slammed, and Misty heard the scuffing of several pairs of boots grinding dirt into the hardwood floor. Bronson made his way into the kitchen with his brothers a few steps behind him. The four men sounded like a mob disassembling after a rally rather than four men coming in from working outside.

"I'll be out in a second," she called from the walk-in pantry. She snatched two spice bottles from the shelf—one of cumin and the other of chili powder—and walked out.

Bronson's crooked grin caused her senses to tingle with excitement.

"Wow. I expected to find a landfill of groceries scattered all over the granite counter." He placed his hands on his hips. "I thought you'd be struggling to find spots for everything we'd picked up today."

"I'm full of all kinds of surprises!" She held a spice jar in each hand six-gun style and twirled them like the men and women in the rodeo did when they wanted the crowd to cheer.

Years of living on the road had made her very resourceful. Spice twirling was one of the qualifications she could add to her résumé.

The 4M Ranch was nothing compared to what she was used to dealing with. She had made the place immaculate. There was no way she could have functioned in all of the male kitchen chaos. She added a few shakes of the spices to the pot then put them away. She had worked herself into a fluster and was a bit queasy, so she hurried to set the table while several pots simmered on the stove. The exhaust fan whirled on high, drowning out any noise.

Bronson chuckled. "You're *are* full of surprises."

His brothers shoved past him and made a beeline over to where the heavenly aroma floated through the air. Lifting the lid of a large stainless steel pot, Reese reached for the slotted spoon resting on the counter and knocked a plastic spice bottle to the floor while Braxton and Radford tugged open the oven door to see what was cooking inside.

Hearing the noise Misty placed her hand on her hips and

barked out, "Stop." Jaw set, she charged over to Reese and yanked the spoon from his hand. "Close that," she commanded, pointing the spoon at Reese who instinctively obeyed, resting the lid in place. "What do you guys think you're doing?"

"We're starving," Radford said with his head still in the oven. Misty placed her hand on his shoulder, pried him away from the oven, and gently shut the door.

"I'd like to volunteer to be your official taste tester." Braxton lifted his hat, and with a dramatic arm-swooping gesture, bowed down in front of her. "At your service."

Reese's eyes pleaded like a puppy begging for scraps from the holiday table. "Me too."

"Misty," Bronson said, "What can I do to help?" He may have been a bit late, but she was getting tired. He wore an expression of guilt, and she sensed he regretted leaving her to put the enormous amount of supplies away.

Misty pursed her lips and then slid them into a sly smile. "I've got this. The only thing I need from you four big, strong men is your taste buds when I'm finished."

"I'm in," Reese fired back.

"Me too," Radford said.

The back door opened and a man took a few steps inside. His pale blue shirt had seen better days—patterned wet stains of dirt and blood covered the sweat-dampened garment. He removed his hat and wiped his head with the soiled cloth he pulled from his back pocket.

"Cast's on and he's resting. I gave him something for pain. Mind if I freshen up in here?" He made eye contact with Misty, then nodded. "Howdy." She gave him a worthwhile grin.

Bronson interjected, "Misty, this here is Doc Harrison." Her smile glued in place, she froze for a second, then pulled the black oven mitt off her hand and extended it.

"My pleasure. I've heard so much about you." Her reaction was stiff and uncomfortable. Most single women in Crystal Cove must drink in the doc's charm and good looks. Dark hair, warm caramel eyes, and a muscular yet slender build. But Misty was afraid to react. Did pregnancy guilt riddle her face? Could he tell her condition?

"Go right ahead. You know the way," Reese said. "Doc has practically lived out at the 4M Ranch since he could talk—working alongside his father who was the town's doctor. He retired when Harrison returned from medical school."

Beads of perspiration formed on the back of her neck and forehead. A wave of nausea hit her in the stomach—hard. Doc Harrison smelled like a barn full of cow manure. As she darted down the hallway, she realized this must be her first bout with morning sickness—except it was the afternoon.

Jeez. How embarrassing!

Even worse, Bronson and his brothers had to have discovered her situation by now. She'd grabbed a hand towel off the counter and run down the hallway into the bathroom, while she'd heaved what little she'd had in her stomach from *that smell*. She pressed the cool damp cloth harder into her face and neck. She wanted to stuff her entire body in the small white hand towel and toss herself into the laundry bin never to be seen again.

It was all Doc Harrison's fault, she snorted in disgust. He'd triggered the repulsive reaction. That one incident had sent her hurtling into the bathroom, retching over the commode. They *had* to know she was pregnant. What would she say? How could she leave with her dignity intact? Would Bronson cancel their deal? Oh, how she needed this job.

There was a light tapping on the door. She didn't have to be a psychic to know who it was. *Bronson.* She fanned her face to cool the color rising in her scorched cheeks.

"Misty, are you all right?" His deep voice stroked her senses and calmed her. How she wished she were. She'd be just fine if they'd all go back outside and let her exit the house in peace. But that would never happen. For some reason, they seemed to genuinely care—not only about what happened to her but, more importantly, everyone else in Crystal Cove.

No, she wasn't all right. She'd never be all right—not here getting cozy at the 4M Ranch. She had to leave— focus the rest of her life on raising her child. There was no room for a man in her future. Getting comfortable at 4M Ranch was a mistake. For one thing, Jim would return, then there was the fair to prepare for…and Beau; she'd eventually have to deal with that situation too. Aww hell, her life was confusing enough without adding the complications of a relationship in the mix.

Beau. He hadn't even crossed her mind once—not since… Well, since she'd raked her eyes all over Bronson. Should she tell Beau? She'd grown up without a father figure. Didn't her child have the right to know their father? She should, at least, give Beau the option to say no to fatherhood, shouldn't she?

Resting her forehead on the old wooden door, she inhaled the scented, grained cedar—how unusual. Her temples pulsated as the craziness of her life swirled around in her head.

"I'm fine. Be out in a minute," she called through the thick wooden door. One look at Doc Harrison, and she would be back in this room, retching up yesterday's lunch. She unlocked the door. The click of the latch echoed off the ceiling as she opened it enough to peer through the crack. Bronson's steely eyes stared back at her. Neither of them said anything for a moment.

"I'm sorry. I don't know what happened."

Bronson chuckled. "I understand. The guys do too."

The McCabe brothers knew her secret—and he was laughing at it—at her! A shiver rippled down her spine, and it made her ill all over again. She closed and locked the door and pressed her forehead against the hard wood. Why her? Why was this happening? She wasn't ready. Not yet. When the town of Crystal Cove learned about her pregnancy, she had wanted it to be on her terms, when she was prepared. Not now. Not like this. Morning sickness in the afternoon—the big red flag. To hell with them.

"Don't be embarrassed. Me and the guys understand how these things happen." He jiggled the doorknob. "Hell, it's happened to each of us at one time or another. We've learned to deal with it and move on. You will too."

Deal with it? Move on? How the heck was she supposed to do that? It was easy for a guy to skip out on a child's life but not a mother.

Normally, a mother didn't abandon her children to dive into a relationship. Well, not too often. Unless she was Marla Summers. The sour memories of her mother's twisted ways tainted Misty's sense of family normalcy.

"I doubt it." There was no way he had morning sickness or the feeling of being watched by an entire town. Besides, he was a man and rules were different for men, weren't they? This may be the twenty-first century, but in this small town, the old double standard still held strong.

She opened the door slightly to find his steel gray gaze and crooked grin peering back at her. Chin held high she flung open the door. At this point, she didn't care what they thought. Her child came first, and he or she was all that mattered. She needed to be able to support herself without relying on anyone's help. Relaxing her shoulders, she straightened her back, and with her head up, she prepared for the assault of inevitable questions.

Suck it up, Misty. Enough of this hormonal sappy crap.

"Excuse me." She pushed past Bronson, marched out into the hallway, and returned to the kitchen. The McCabe brothers, minus the doctor, worked to salvage the meal she'd left simmering on the stove.

The gravy for the pot roast!

"Did it burn?" she asked while shoving her hands into a pair of oven mitts. She slid the hot gravy pot off the burner. "I'll take it from here," she ordered, holding up a hand, signaling them back. The brothers did as they were told. She shot a glance over to the doorway where Bronson watched her with amusement in his eyes. *Seriously? To hell with him.* Her blood pressure kicked up a few points. He found her illness entertaining. He hadn't changed. None of them had. Why, she'd bet the four of them found her situation comical—like when they were kids. Only this time things were different. She had her baby to think about and nothing they could say or do would take away the happiness deep in her heart—like when she imagined the life the two of them would have. Boy or girl, this child would be her entire world. No men allowed.

She went to the oven to check on the pot roast. With a gloved hand, she lifted the lid. It was done. The cast-iron Dutch oven pot weighed a ton. She pulled it out, struggling to get it over to the trivet nearby.

"You okay?" Grabbing a towel, Radford tried to pry the hot pot from her oven mitted hands without burning himself in the process. Misty carefully handed over the pot roast she'd removed from the oven. The silence was deafening; all she could do was shrug. Words bounced around in her head but couldn't make their way out of her mouth. She wanted to clear the air and explain.

Reese place a gentle hand on her arm. "Don't be embarrassed. Sweat and blood in the heat have a way of making even a man with a strong stomach pitch his insides." He looked into her eyes with understanding. "Why, Jim even passed out once. Isn't that right, guys?"

"The doc has had that effect on all of us at one point," Braxton said with a wink from across the room, then turned his attention to the doorway where their old friend cleared his throat.

Doc Harrison had appeared from around the corner. "Aww, guys. You hurt my feelings. I'm insulted." He entered from the hallway into the kitchen, his dark hair damp, dressed in clean jeans and a fresh shirt. "Thanks for the use of your shower." He grinned and walked over to the refrigerator. "Mind if I help myself to a water?"

Doc opened the refrigerator and pulled out a bottle, not waiting for an answer. He tapped the door closed with an elbow, twisted off the cap, and the tossed it in the trash can across the room.

"'Course not. I owe you." Bronson stood with his arms folded and rocked back on his heels. "Misty just got her initiation into the 4M Ranch." He looked at her with concern. "I hope this doesn't mean you're going to change your mind."

Misty watched the exchange, feeling uncomfortable and out of place with all eyes on her. She had the urge to leave before they continued their conversation. "No," she said slowly. She was positive the doctor must realize she was pregnant. How could he not?

"You rushed over here and helped us, Doc. Can I interest you in something to eat?" Bronson dropped his arms at his side, pulled out a chair, and sat down at the table. "This kitchen smells better and better with Misty's cooking." He knit his eyebrows together, then directed his attention toward her. "Do you want to go home?"

Did she? Heck yeah—and no. She had so much work to do at the 4M Ranch and the house—her house—was a mess and there was her business arrangement with Arlene. She had to juggle so much and needed to find a sense of balance. This job was what she needed to jumpstart her future, and she wouldn't give Bronson or his brothers an excuse to replace her and hire someone else.

Bronson had agreed to supply her with everything she needed for the fair. Walking out on them now, no matter what they thought about her, would be a major setback. "I'll be fine," she murmured. There was an overwhelming list of things to do, so when would she find the time to work on her house? Never. At this rate, even if she had the money, she'd never finish the repairs. Stay focused. One day at a time.

"So, Misty, what brings you to town after all this time?

Huh? Now the doc started an inquisition.

"I'd been away for so long." *Pregnant after a one-night stand and decided to come home to my grandmother who passed away, but you probably already know all of that.* "A spur of the moment thing."

Doc pierced her with a stare. "It's unfortunate you didn't decide to come back a few months sooner, *before* your grandmother passed." His emphasis on the word "before" made her shift uncomfortably.

Debra Fisk

Up until now she hadn't had the courage to ask anyone about the details. The hair on the back of her neck began to rise. What had he heard? What did he know? Or was she paranoid? Oh, somebody give her some answers.

Doc Harrison offered, "Your grandmother died suddenly even for someone with pancreatic cancer."

"Pancreatic cancer?" she murmured the words aloud. How sad and depressing and awful that her grandmother had died alone—in pain—with cancer. Even if it had been quick, she'd have been there to comfort her. Doc Harrison's news left her grief-stricken. She pulled out a chair from around the table and collapsed in it. Instead of being there when her grandmother needed her, she'd allowed her mother's lies to keep them apart. If only she could go back in time, relive the moment she'd decided to leave and change her decision. Her life would be completely different now. One thing was for sure, she could have erased the past ten years of enduring hellacious conditions.

Levi Gilligan tapped his pencil on his yellow pad, shaking his head. "I hate to say this, young lady. I'm afraid there's a lot of work that needs to be done." With a frown, he scribbled feverishly along the paper with his wide carpenter's pencil, pausing only to glance up at the roof.

Shielding her eyes from the afternoon sun, Misty followed his gaze, not sure what he was referring to exactly—the roof or the entire house. She was too afraid to ask, worried about the answer she might receive.

"Can't you patch it?" she asked, biting her lower lip while a sick sensation rested in the center of her stomach. This wasn't the news she had hoped for, and she dreaded hearing his full assessment. This day wasn't going very well at all. She blew out a long, slow breath. Things could be worse—much worse—but things could be a little better too, she rationalized. This cemented why she needed to set the wheels in motion to win the state fair prize money.

"A lot of work to be done." His frown deepened, and she couldn't make out his eyes behind the dark glasses. For a man over sixty, he'd stalked up the ladder with forceful purpose in the afternoon Florida sun and stood on the roof for nearly twenty minutes—all without passing out. Misty had started to get overheated and light-headed watching him—afraid he might fall and roll off onto the weed-filled lawn.

It was the third time today she had heard those words. Once from Clem Shay from Dillard's Auto Garage, and twice from Levi Gilligan, the local handyman. Now, as Levi stood next to her, figuring out the cost of the suggested repairs, she realized how dire her situation really was. She had to win that prize money. This house needed a lot of TLC, and she wanted to give it every bit of the love it deserved. The happiest moments of her life had been spent in this house. They were the only happy moments she'd shared as a family. The three of them were a small family, but they had been a family once.

Well, it would be the two of them now, and that was all she needed here, right? She didn't need any man in her life, not Bronson or Beau. She thought about Beau again. A nagging part of her conscience told her to contact him. Then what? What would he say? She imagined all sorts of replies from "*marry me*" to "*whose baby is it*" to "*I don't even know you, do I?*" Handsome, rugged and sexy, Beau was popular with the ladies, and they *did* love him. But did she? No. Not one bit. Would she be able to make a life with him? No. Well—maybe—for the sake of the baby. They could try. Hell, this heat was making her delirious!

Beads of sweat poured out all over Levi's face, and she offered, "Let's step inside into the cool air to talk. I'll make both of us a fresh glass of iced tea."

Levi nodded and motioned with his arm for her to lead the way. His blue button-down shirt was peppered with huge damp patches that stuck to his chest in several places. He followed behind her up the front porch and through the screen door. He smelled like sweat and musty shirt fabric. Enough to make her almost retch.

Summer Heat

"Man oh man," she heard Levi mumble when she opened the wooden door. A blast of ice-cold air was a welcome relief as she made her way into the kitchen. Amazed, Levi said, "At least the air-conditioner unit was one of the few things new in the house."

She went over to the overhead cabinet and removed two glasses. "Is it?" Well, at least there wasn't a chance of it breaking down. One less thing to worry about. She walked over to the refrigerator, removing the pitcher of iced tea from inside. "Sugar? Lemon?"

"Please."

It was so hot out she filled each glass to the brim with ice then fixed Levi's tea and turned to hand it to him. Daydreaming—she searched for ways to solve her money problems and came up short, half listening to what Levi told her.

"Evelyn replaced it two years ago after a storm swept through here," he said, taking the glass from her. "I put it in as a favor. Your grandmother was a sweet, kind lady." She watched Levi as his eyes began to redden. A few flecks of tears touched the corner of his lashes. "When my wife passed, Evelyn cooked meals and brought them over to my house. I hear you've inherited her cooking skills. Making good food is a gift."

A gift? Somehow she hadn't thought of it that way. But now that Levi mentioned it, cooking was very therapeutic. The preparation was a way of calming her nerves or working out problems in her head. She enjoyed watching people eat the things she prepared. Love was an essential ingredient in each dish or baked item she made. People came together over meals. They enjoyed each other's company, shared their day over dinner.

So often, she had eaten alone in silence. She longed for a loving family to share her life with. Back when she still lived with her mother on the road, a bottle of vodka or any other type of alcohol was what her mother had called a meal. Those "family dinners" consisted of conversations about Misty's faults. With a sharp, drunken tongue, her mother was quick to tell everyone else what was wrong with them, but refused look at herself in the mirror. The McCabe brothers had what she wanted one day: a loving family. Even though their parents were gone, they had each other. She would have her baby. A broad smile filled her face.

"I'm happy to watch people enjoy eating the meals I prepare." She planned for her baby to be raised on all-natural baby food that she prepared at home. She had heard of people steaming vegetable and placing them in a food processor, something she didn't have but could save up for by the time she would need it. It made sense, a healthy choice for the baby and a financial savings to boot.

"Have you tried one of my meals from the cafe?"

Everything she cooked went to the Lakeside Inn, except what she made at the McCabe's.

"Nah, not yet." He downed the remainder of his tea. "Well, I gotta go to another appointment, so I'll get back to you with the cost, and let me know if you need anything else." He stood up and was out the door in a hurry.

"Thank you," she called after him, wondering if something she'd said had upset him. Not five minutes later, she heard the sound of a truck arriving outside and went to the window.

Did Levi forget something? No. Bronson made his way up the front porch. Her heart skipped around in her chest. Feeling giddy like a schoolgirl, she yanked opened the door. "I heard you pull up."

"I heard you had Dillard's out here. Levi too. Thought I'd come by and see is anything wrong?" His wicked grin fired an arrow of heat straight to her heart. He removed his hat as he stepped inside. "I did lend you a truck. Are you planning on backing out of our agreement?"

His skeptical face made her wary. Could he read her so well he picked up she'd contemplated quitting yesterday? She hoped not.

Bronson wanted to kick himself the second he stepped into the old Summers place. Why the heck was he even there? He studied Misty with suspicion, waiting for an answer. Her face was riddled with guilt over something, but he'd be damned if he knew what it was. Dropping by unannounced had seemed like a good idea at the time. He wanted to get some type of a clue as to what she was up to. Would she tell him the truth?

He scanned the room from where he stood. The house was as dated on the inside as it was on the outside. A pang of sadness tweaked in his chest. Misty had left her grandmother's belongings exactly as she'd found them. The place smelled of fresh lemon and furniture polish. From what he could see, she'd been busy cleaning months of dust and grime. The faded draperies in the living room had been freshened and rehung over the windows. In the corner was a big easy chair. Evelyn's knitting still sat beside it, her reading glasses and a book left opened waiting for her return. Clearly Misty was still in mourning and unwilling to make the house her own. He understood the process of grief all too well. He'd been through it each time he'd lost a parent.

"I didn't expect you to come by," she said, her voice higher than usual.

His eyes snapped in her direction. A honey-kissed curl dangled in the center of her forehead, and he wanted to reach out and touch it. The dark blue depths pulled him in, and he waited for her to answer his question.

She took a deep breath, then said, "No, nothing like that. I wanted a true assessment of what needs to be done to make this home grand like it once was." She turned her head and looked behind her, as if she'd added something else to the long list of repairs. The curl in the center of her forehead bounced. "I'm trying to get an idea what I'm up against." Her face scrunched up with worry. Her T-shirt slipped off her shoulder, and he wanted to trace a line to her jaw with his lips.

Instead, he said, "I can understand that." He chided himself for always thinking the worst of her, but in an instant, he forgave the thought. After all, this was Marla Summers's daughter. Hot and sexy didn't work for him, and Misty was both of those.

Hell, he didn't need any other excuses. Women were not a good fit in his life. After all, Delilah took his love, manipulated his emotions, and erased every bit of trust he once had in women. Misty could never be a part of his life even if she were perfect. He'd sworn never to let another woman into his heart, and so far, he'd succeeded. He began to regret stopping by. Sure, he'd hooked up on weekends looking for fun occasionally with a woman not interested in a relationship—just a good time but nothing serious. The day Delilah skipped out and left was the day he'd decided no more relationships for him.

He made up a flimsy excuse for his visit. "I wanted to be sure you felt comfortable cooking for the workers' appreciation dinner. It's in one week. You can't back out now." With a head tilt, he waggled his eyebrows in a half joking gesture. He didn't want to scare her off or let on how desperate he really was. No way would he give her that kind of power over him.

She took a few steps back and looked at him through thick dark lashes. "The deal stands." Her tone was firm and strong.

Convinced she meant business, he winked and said, "Then my work here is done." The air conditioner blasted cold air but to him the room seemed a little too hot for comfort.

"I have a few more things to figure out here, then I'll be by to start dinner." She brushed the curl away from her forehead—the one he'd fought so hard not to touch. He reached out and brushed her cheek with his thumb without realizing why he did it.

"Anything I can help you with?" The words tumbled out of his mouth before he could stop them, and he cringed. What was wrong with him? He had work back at the ranch and shouldn't be here wasting time. *Pull yourself away.*

She paused with a smile. "I appreciate the offer, but no."

"Then I'll see you this evening." He nodded and placed his hat on his head, eager to be on his way. His blood pumped anxiously to get the hell outta there. He shouldn't be alone with her. It was obvious it had been too long since he'd bedded a woman.

Debra Fisk

"Well, have you entered yet?" Arlene pierced Misty with a long, hard stare over her glasses. Queasiness hit Misty in the stomach. Was it the pregnancy or the pressure of Arlene's scrutiny? She looked around the empty cafe; it was cool inside and the lights were dim, a direct contrast to the blazing sun that tried to scorch the tinted windows.

"What's up?" Motioning with her head at the empty cafe.

For a Friday afternoon, the people were sparse, so why had Arlene called her down here to bring more food? Misty had been baking bread, cakes, and smoking more barbecue back at her house when Arlene called saying it was an emergency, that she needed whatever was finished.

Annoyed, she dropped the heavy tray on the counter with a slam, and a trickle of sauce sloshed over the side, forming a puddle of spicy brown glaze in the shape of a heart. Cute. It made her think of Bronson for a moment. Silly daydreams. Picking up a napkin, she automatically began to wipe it up, to erase any trace of sauce or him.

"I thought you called me down here for more food." The sticky substance had now adhered to her fingers. Peeling off bits of torn napkin cemented to the tips, she pushed Arlene for an answer. "Well?"

Arlene's expression darkened. "I did, but you need to enter if you're going to win the grand prize." Arlene slid the tray over so she had room to rest her elbows on the faded Formica. "Well, don't bother now."

"Why not?"

Make up your mind, Arlene, one minute enter—the next, don't. Could Arlene confuse her any more than she already had?

Arlene pulled a cigarette out from behind her ear and tapped the end on the counter. "I've already paid your registration, that's why," Arlene spat in a tone of disappointment. She frowned and Misty felt like a schoolgirl being scolded by the teacher.

"You did?" Not what she'd expected—at all.

"Yup. How are you supposed to win if you don't enter?"

She could hear the irritation in Arlene's voice.

Misty battled the sticky fingers. "But why?" She'd been saving up for it. She could pay her own way and didn't want to be known as the town's charity case. Especially once they found out she was pregnant. They'd feel betrayed. She could imagine the commotion it would cause once they learned her secret. Arlene cared enough to offer her help, imagine when she discovered Misty didn't trust her enough to confide in her. She struggled every day with the guilt of being what she considered dishonest. Others might call it being private, but to Misty she felt as though she was deceiving people who really cared about her and each other. That was what small communities were all about. Crystal Cove had grown on her and so had the people.

A smile tugged at the corner of Arlene's mouth. "I figured you could use the help." Her sheepish expression made the hairs on the back of Misty's neck begin to rise. Her spidey senses began to tingle on high alert. Arlene seemed a bit cryptic to her. Was there something else?

Misty pressed a big fake smile across her face. "Thank you."

Was she being paranoid again? Maybe. She stared back down and continued to unsuccessfully rip off the flakes of sticky dried paper.

Misty looked the older woman square in the eye. "I'll

Debra Fisk

make you proud, Arlene."

"I know you will." With a smile of satisfaction, Arlene
lifted the foil cover off the tray and inhaled. "Delicious.
You're making quite a name for yourself around here.
People are callin' from two towns away for takeout."

Two towns? Really?

"If this keeps up, you're gonna to have to tell those
McCabes to find someone else to cook." Arlene smacked
her hand down on the counter as if the deal had been
already finalized. "Want me to call them right now?" she
offered.

"No." Panic caused her heart to kick up a few notches.
There was no way Misty could break her deal with
Bronson, at least not until the picnic was over. Right?
That was something she would worry about later. At the
moment, she had to juggle several jobs. If only she could
divide her time evenly between Bronson and Arlene.
Somehow she'd squeeze in her plan for the fair. Time was
not on her side and the weight of responsibility crushed
her breathing.

Arlene's voice softened. "Is there something you want to
tell me? Are you in some kind of trouble?"

Heck no.

"Tell you?" A long, nervous overdone laugh ensued.
Waving her arms about, trying to free just one crumb of

torn napkin from her hands. "You know more about my family past than I do. No, I'm not in any *trouble*."

She didn't consider having her baby *trouble*. The timing was not the greatest, but reflecting on the situation, she might never have returned to Crystal Cove or discovered her grandmother had passed if it hadn't been for the pregnancy. Tears started to well up every time she thought of how she'd missed, by a few months, seeing her one more time. Add to that was the guilt of how her grandmother had died alone.

She sighed. "I arrived here too late to spend time with her." Her emotions got the best of her. She needed to call Carly. She'd been putting it off for weeks. At least if she could spill her guts to her over the phone, she might feel better.

And that was when the tears began to fall. Arlene flipped her a clean paper napkin from the stack. With a weak smile, Misty took it, dabbed her eyes, and blew her nose. What a mess. Did women always cry at the drop of a hat when they were pregnant?

Misty heard the door creak open and the light sound of high-heeled boots click across the solid wooden floor behind her. Yanking a few more napkins from the pile, she tried to clean her face and dry her tears the best she could. There was only one person who wore high-heeled boots in town in the middle of the day. Misty looked up, and in the reflection of Arlene's glasses, she saw…

Darla.

"Hey. You're just in time. Your order's ready." Arlene's voice echoed in the empty restaurant. "Nice and hot too."

"Yum. I can smell the goodness from here." Darla walked up next to Misty. "How are you, hon? Everything all right?" Darla stood before her, sparkling with her glowing blonde hair, glittery eye shadow, and iridescent pearl lip-gloss. She could have been on the cover of any glamour magazine instead of being a socialite around the quaint town of Crystal Cove. She placed her arm around Misty and gave her a squeeze.

"I'm fine. Great. Really."

Scanning Darla, Misty marveled how Darla had such a sense of fashion. The patterns on her boots matched the pattern on her dress. Her entire ensemble—earrings, bracelets, and purse—were all color-coordinated. Fascinating. How many pairs of boots did Darla own?

Beautiful, smart, sexy, and yet, as sweet as she was, Darla was still unmarried and unattached and her sister was not. How could that be? The men of Crystal Cove must drool as she walked by. Wasn't she interested in a relationship?

"Wow. You look amazing. I love your sense of style." With an acknowledgment of defeat, she mumbled, "Somehow I missed getting that gene," being honest about the disappointment in her lack of style. There was a whole lot Misty had missed out on—like a father in her life. Would her baby yearn to know about Beau? Tears betrayed her for the second time, and she felt like a blubbering fool in front of the two women.

She could see confusion on their faces. Neither one of them understood her emotional roller coaster of mood swings. Darla wore a sympathetic pout, and Arlene frowned through pursed lips. A sharp pang of hunger squeeze Misty's stomach. That must be it. She hadn't eaten a morsel of food since breakfast. Using the smoker outside in the heat and baking bread and pastries inside the house since before dawn had allowed her energy well to run dry.

"I'm sorry to ask you, Arlene. Can you make me something from the kitchen? I haven't eaten anything since I cooked breakfast for Bronson and his brothers."

She had made them a breakfast casserole with the hope that they would eat the leftovers the next day; too bad they'd finished the remainder for a midday snack before lunch. She'd have to work something else out if she wanted to accomplish all of her goals. Later tonight, she would revise her strategy and needs on paper. A list would help her to stay on course. If she stuck to a plan and didn't get sidetracked, she'd hit all of her marks for her progress.

"You got it. Have a seat. Darla, would you like something?" Arlene got up off her stool from behind the counter, walked over to the bar, and grabbed two glasses and held them up. "Tea? Lemonade? Half and half?"

"Sure. I'll have an iced tea with a bit of lemonade added." Darla smiled and batted eyelids so glittery they could start a fire from reflecting sunlight outdoors. Of course, she'd only want an iced tea blend. Misty felt like she could eat an entire cow. Hungry, weepy, and grouchy —not a pleasant combination. Maybe she was being too hard on herself.

Darla paused, deep in thought, as if this decision was going to solve the world's problems. "Half and half." She nodded in affirmation. It was settled.

More relaxed, Misty called out, "Unsweetened tea with extra lemon." She wasn't being fair to Darla right now, but given her hungry, moody pregnant state, she couldn't help it.

They moved to a nearby table, and Arlene set down their drinks along with two menus. The build your own Angus burger jumped out when Misty flipped the cover open— with a double order of jalapeño cheese french fries. *Yum!*

"I'll have the build your own burger, medium-well, cheddar, pickles, grilled onion, bacon, with a double order of jalapeño cheese fries." She didn't care she over-ordered; it sounded too good to pass up.

"Oh, that sounds good. I'll have the same." Darla flipped her menu closed, grinning at Misty. "I figure, what the heck, I can't sit here and pass that up."

Arlene scratched the order onto her pad and walked into the kitchen. Misty could here Arlene talking to her longtime love interest, Moe, while he cooked their order.

Darla sipped on the straw of the lemonade and tea blend. "So, what are your plans?"

Startled, Misty missed her glass and dropped the lemon she was squeezing on the table. "Whatever do you mean?" Did Darla suspect she was pregnant? Maybe she shouldn't have ordered the double order of jalapeño fries. Had that given her away?

Darla set her glass down and leaned in closer. "I mean for your future. You know—work-wise. Jim will probably come back eventually and then where will you be?"

Silence.

With her head bobbing, Darla said, "Jobless right?"

She did have a point, and Misty hadn't wanted to dwell on the Jim factor. She liked cooking for the McCabe brothers. She was pretty sure Jim wasn't planning on returning any time soon, but what if he did? Her ravishing hunger dissipated with the reminder of her worries, but this opened up the opportunity to ask Darla, in a tactful way, about her future and why she wasn't married.

Changing the subject, she said, "I know you don't need to work. Do you mind me asking, why haven't you married?"

"I don't mind at all. It's not for me."

Not for her? Interesting. Misty held out her arms. "I mean you're smart, stunning, and have a head on your shoulders. What's not for you? You could have your pick of Crystal Cove's eligible men—or anywhere else for that matter."

Darla shrugged. "I've a great life. Why mess it up with a man telling me what to do?" She laid it out matter-of-factly, and Misty had to agree she had a point. That was why Misty hadn't contacted Beau to tell him about the baby. She didn't want to answer to a man either. She'd witnessed firsthand how men had controlled her mother's life, and there was no way a man would control hers.

"I agree." They laughed and toasted their glasses of tea with a good solid clink.

"Look at my sister Audrey. She's crazy about Justin, but her life revolves around his wants and the baby's. She always puts herself last. That's not what I want out of life." Darla's cell phone buzzed with a text, and she messaged the person back.

"Besides, I think I'm going to open a women's boutique." She looked up, dreamy, and continued, "With high-fashion boots, dresses, and jewelry to match the clothing."

Why would she want to be tied down when she didn't need the money? Working in retail was hard. Although with her family background, she'd probably hire someone to run it for her.

"I'm going to call it Southern Lady Rider." Darla beamed. "Isn't that an awesome name?" She motioned with her hand in the air, saying the words again, "Southern Lady Rider. In lights."

The door to the cafe jerked opened and Misty glanced over to see whose heavy boots scuffed the wooden floor. *Bronson.* She glanced back to Darla, trying to avoid his gaze when he spotted her. She raked her fingers through her long, tangled ponytail in a feeble attempt to repair the disheveled mess. Next to Darla, she looked like a bag lady on the side of the road.

He walked over to their table and stared down at Misty. "I've been trying to reach you." Something in his voice sounded urgent. Her heart fluttered around in her chest, and she felt light-headed from being hungry and anxious at the same time. Her blood pumped in an erratic rhythm in her veins because of his closeness. In the wall mirror, she could see her reflection. Heat stained her cheeks pink, and she removed her cold hands from around the iced tea glass and rested them on her face. She swore she heard them sizzle.

"Is something wrong?" she asked, still trying to refresh her warm cheeks with her hands. Why did he have this effect on her? *Because he's hot; that's why.* Handsome, kind—a respectable man. He would never be interested in someone like her with a sordid family history. No, someone like Darla would be perfect for him. She could see the two of them as a couple. She wondered why they weren't an item. The muscular rancher and the heiress to the retail chain. Two of the oldest and founding families in Crystal Cove united.

"Hey, Bronson." Darla flipped her hair, then took a hard draw on her straw. Her gaze snapped back and forth between Misty and Bronson. She tilted her head to study their moves.

He replied, "Darla." Bronson returned his gaze to Misty. "I tried to call you a few times, but there was no answer." He pulled out a chair from another table, spun it around, and straddled it. "At your house and on your cell. I was worried."

He looked so strong and tan, and when he took off his hat, she wanted to run her fingers through his thick messed-up hair to try to fix it. His eyes twinkled with mischief in the dim lighting, and she wondered why he was looking for her.

"My cell is dead right now, and I was outside manning the smoker with a rush order for Arlene."

"One of our dogs is about to have puppies. I thought you might like to be there to see them born." His grin was from ear to ear, and she slipped a little deeper into the "like" mode. Which wasn't hard to do. She'd better watch and be careful before she was in too deep and over her head.

"That's so sweet." Darla, who'd remained virtually invisible up until now, added her two cents. "What breed of dog is it? Mutt?"

Bronson gave her a frown, but ignored Darla's question. "Whenever we have an addition to the ranch, I try to be there to welcome our newest members into the family, large and small."

Would he be there to welcome her baby into the ranch family? Doubtful.

The one thing she had learned, spending time at the ranch, was how family was at the core of their values. Whether it was a ranch hand, employee, or animal, the McCabe brothers took care of their own.

Arlene popped out from the kitchen. "Here you go, girls." She carried the stacked plates on one arm and grinned when she saw Bronson. For her age, Arlene, with her strong arms and toned legs, was still in great shape, able to carry the weight of the heavy platters. "Hey, Bronson, you want a drink or a bite to eat?"

Misty could guess his answer before he spoke. She got the feeling the McCabe brothers were always hungry.

"Sure would."

Bingo.

He smiled up at Arlene, and Misty thought she would faint from hunger and his sexy grin —a deadly combination. He looked at Darla's and Misty's burgers with a side of smothered cheese fries and pointed to Misty's plate. "I'll take one of those."

Misty grabbed a knife and cut her burger in half, to prevent shoving the entire thing in her mouth. She controlled her eating frenzy by taking a few small nibbles of a fry, but then began to stuff her face with the burger while Darla stabbed at her fries with a fork and took minuscule bites.

"Well?" Darla stopped eating holding her fork in midair. Her arched eyebrows and pursed lips caused Misty to shift uncomfortably. Darla was all business while she waited for Misty to answer.

"Well what?" Holding the burger, about to take a bite, she waited for a clue from Darla. The smell of sautéed onions, cheese, and bacon made her mouth water, and she struggled not to sink her teeth into it again.

Darla rolled her eyes in disgust. "Do you want to work at my boutique? I think you'd be perfect for the job."

Bronson spoke up. "What boutique? What are you talking about? Misty has a job at the 4M and here catering for

Arlene." He rocked forward on two legs of the chair. "She's not interested." Then he folded his arms across his chest and balanced the chair on two legs while he spoke.

Whoa there, cowboy. Exactly why she didn't need a man to complicate things. The men she'd been around automatically took control of a woman's life, forcing her to do what they said. No…that wasn't the future she imagined. Not now. Not ever.

"She has a job with you now, but when Jim gets back, she'll be out the door with no way to support herself." Leave it Darla to point out the horror of her life in public. Thankfully there was no one in the diner to hear Darla's broadcast. Misty suddenly lost the urge to tear into her food and lick her plate clean.

Would Bronson let her go that easily? Misty didn't want to wait and see. She understood Bronson wanted to help her, but Darla was right. What if Jim returned tomorrow? What would happen to her then? If Arlene hadn't paid for Misty's entry fee for the fair, would she have really entered? Winning the fair was her ticket to independence and financial freedom. She'd better get her priorities in order. Living a fantasy life at the 4M didn't pay the bills or create a future to support her baby. Men were all talk and little action. She'd learned that the hard way.

"That's not going to happen," Bronson said firmly. The chair came down on the floor with a slam. "When Jim does return, I'm sure Misty and I can come to some type of agreement." He turned and looked at her. "Right?" His fingers gripped the back of the chair, waiting for her reply. Maybe...if the agreement suited his needs, but she wanted to have a choice, not be pinned into a corner or forced to work in a job she didn't enjoy.

She hadn't seen Bronson this agitated before. Did it have something to do with Darla? Or something else? She'd worry about that later. Misty cleared her throat. "We have time. Southern Lady Rider isn't anywhere near opened, and Jim is still traveling, enjoying his new bride." Anything could happen long before Jim's return, like Misty's pregnancy being discovered and the repercussions from that, or she could win the fair and start her own business of bottling her barbecue sauce. The recipe wasn't quite ready but she was so close to having a winner. She wanted to wow the judges, the crowd, and blow the competition away with her recipe.

Arlene returned with Bronson's plate and placed if before him with a glass of tea. Arlene pulled up a chair next to them. The whiff of cigarette smoke followed her every move. Misty noticed that in her condition it made her queasy.

"First, we have the workers' appreciation picnic." Bronson lifted a reminding eyebrow. How could she forget? It was the main reason he'd made the deal with her in the first place. She wasn't about to mess this up. She wanted to thank him and his brothers for the opportunity they'd given her by cooking an outrageous barbecue for all of the 4M Ranch.

"What's going on?" Arlene asked, clearly puzzled by the bit of tension the four of them could cut with a steak knife. "I leave for five minutes and you kids can't get along," she joked.

Misty blurted out, "Darla's going to open a boutique. She asked me to work for her when Jim returns." Talk about mouth running on. Bronson gave her a surprised smile, and her face betrayed her, sizzling with heat. Not that she'd accept the position, but at this point, she had to keep all of her options open.

"When is Jim coming back?" Arlene's face wore a concerned look. She stretched out her legs on another chair and rested her back up against the supporting wall.

"We don't know," Bronson said honestly. "I know he will, but he picked a hell of a time to do it and without warning."

"Must be love…" Darla joked and started to hum some silly love song.

Arlene chimed in. "Must be."

Bronson scowled at their jokes, his eyebrows drawn in a stoic look.

Misty could see a hint of worry in his eyes. She worked on finishing her burger and fries and ate more than she would've thought before pushing her dish away. "I'm finished." Oh so finished, in more ways than one. She had to get back to the house so she could work on the barbecue sauce recipe. She asked Bronson, "Did you pick up the remainder of the supplies and reserve the activity tents for the kids?"

"Everything is all lined up. I have my brothers keeping the land clear so the only thing they need to do is set up the tables and chairs and create a safe swimming hole for the younger children. I hope this picnic isn't too overwhelming for you. I've got plenty of hands ready to pitch in and help." They'd been hosting this picnic for years, so Misty knew they'd have everything under control.

She smiled. "I'm sure it will be fine. Well, ladies, and Bronson, I have to get back home. Will I see you all tomorrow?" Misty pushed out her chair, annoyed that she couldn't stay longer, but the smoker called for her to check on the meat that should be about finished by now.

Bronson looked at her, disappointed. "What about the puppies?" He wiped his hands on a napkin as he stood, having inhaled his burger in record time. A smile slipped across her face at how amusing it was to see a strong, muscular man, one who stood over six feet tall, act like a seven-year-old boy when it came to puppies.

"I'll be over as soon as I'm finished." She wanted to wash her face and change her clothes too, to get rid the scent of hickory and smoke. Having eaten enough for three people, she had plenty of energy to tackle her list problems and solutions.

On the drive back to her house, Misty daydreamed about Bronson and his family. She tried to imagine what it was like growing up in a loving household surrounded by siblings. To have two parents who loved each other, not a mother addicted to alcohol and to loving men who considered women a disposable item. It was hard to imagine her mother and her grandmother were related. They were polar opposites. Her grandmother was a church-going woman, widowed young and never remarried.

Her grandmother once told her that the day she lost her husband a part of her died inside until she had Marla. Growing up without a father affected Marla in a way. She looked for male love and attention. Something clicked off inside of her even though she was very young. She fell in love with a young man at school, but he was never interested in her. Feeling rejected, she went out of her way to get his attention, but failed. Later as she grew older, she sought comfort in alcohol and men—young or old, she didn't care. Her newfound sex addiction had embarrassed Evelyn Summers and had resulted in Misty, but Evelyn was never embarrassed of her granddaughter.

She made sure Misty understood she was loved more than anything in the world. Inheriting the house was her final gift of love, and Misty cherished this home. She sat in the driveway and envisioned the repairs completed and the house restored to the way it once was. Her baby would live in this home surrounded by love. Would the love of one parent be enough?

Bronson hadn't planned on his border collie having puppies. Not now…not ever. She'd begun showing a few weeks ago. The McCabe brothers handled their animals responsibly, making sure all dogs were either spayed or neutered. So now the question was which male dog could be the father. This unexpected litter of puppies had become a very special miracle to Bronson and his brothers. Reese had built a whelping box and they had moved it into the large laundry room off the kitchen. One thing Bronson remembered from a litter as a child was that puppies were much more work than kittens. They required feedings every two hours in the beginning, and you had to be there to help the mother and make sure she was able to nurse them all. The first two weeks were critical, and in a large litter, it wasn't uncommon to lose one or two. Hopefully they wouldn't have to face the loss of a pup.

Lady was panting hard and Reese had called Doc Harrison to come over in case there were complications. Since no one knew what dog fathered these pups, there was a chance they could be too large for her to deliver without a C-section.

"Doc Harrison is on his way but he said to remind you he's not a vet." Reese bent down and scratched Lady behind her ears. She rested her head on a pillow, looking uncomfortable and pathetic.

"Did you remind him that Lady's more than a dog; she's part of our family?" Bronson asked. Reese laughed and collapsed on the large pillows he'd placed outside of the whelping box for them to sit on.

"No. He knows she's family. He's trying to give you a hard time." Reese stretched out onto the jumbo pillows and flopped his arm over his eyes.

Bronson felt responsible for Lady's distress. He shouldn't have taken the shelter's word she'd been fixed. Somehow they'd been mistaken, and Lady now paid the price. Not to mention they had to find homes for eight to ten puppies. Not a simple task.

The back door opened and Lady perked up, lifted her head, and barked.

"Doc?" Bronson called.

"No, it's me," he heard Misty reply. The sound of her light footsteps on the kitchen floor echoed as she walked over to the laundry area and stood in the doorway. Bronson could smell Misty's lemon vanilla fragrance when she stepped into the room. Her hair was damp and she wore an adorable lavender shorts outfit with a matching ribbon in her hair. Her skin glowed, and she looked beautiful with hardly any makeup on. She had a natural beauty. A fresh, clean wholesome look. He gazed down into her dark blue eyes then focused on her full pink lips and wanted to place a kiss on them. Something tugged at his heart, and though his head said, *"Don't even think about it,"* and he remembered Delilah and the fact Misty was a *Summers,* he dismissed it. He wanted to kiss those lips; he wanted to wrap his arms around her. And he wanted to feel her legs around his hips. He wanted to kiss her and hear her moan his name. He reached for her hand, and she placed it in his. A perfect fit. A sudden jolt of electrical current ran through him. His head screamed, *"You're mine."* Still holding her hand, he sat and pulled her down next to him. She leaned beside Lady alongside the box. He placed his arm around Misty while she stroked Lady's soft fur in comfort.

"Before you know it, you're going to be surrounded by beautiful puppies." Her voice soothed. She tilted her head and looked at Bronson. "How long does it take?"

A valid question. "Several hours. It depends on the number of puppies. The average litter is eight to ten. So we're looking at that many hours more or less." Lady shifted uncomfortably and let out a soft howl. Her labored breathing deepened, and Bronson wondered what the heck was taking Doc Harrison so long. "Reese, call the doc now. Find out where he is," he commanded. What if the puppies were too large for her to pass naturally? What if she needed a C-section? He racked his brain, trying to think of any way he could help Lady.

Rubbing his eyes, Reese rolled to his side and sat up. "Relax he'll be here."

"Why don't you call a vet?" Misty questioned. She brushed Lady's fur with her hand. Lady calmed down, soothed by Misty's touch.

"He's on vacation," Bronson answered. "There's only one in town."

"I take it you've been through this before?" Misty asked Reese. She stroked Lady's head to make her comfortable.

"Not since we were kids. We'd rather rescue our domesticated animals from a local shelter than breed them." The poor animal shelters had beautiful animals waiting to be adopted. People always thought they were mutts but there were a lot of purebred dogs in the shelter as well.

Misty's voice rose a few notches. "Isn't there someone else in town who can help?"

The back door opened and heavy boots thudded toward them.

"Doc?" Bronson called. This time Lady didn't move. Instead, she closed her eyes and whimpered.

"Yeah. I'm here," Doc Harrison replied, filling the doorway. "I still don't know what the heck you expect me to do. I'm not a vet. Did you forget the patients I treat are human?"

Bronson stood and offered his hand to Misty to help her up. "No, but you're the closest thing we've got." Unless there was some kind of other emergency, Doc was going to stay here to help Lady if she needed surgery.

Doc bent down and examined Lady. Shaking his head, he said, "Yup, she's in labor."

Reese and Bronson exchanged glances, then Bronson rolled his eyes. "Very funny."

Misty spoke in a soft voice. "Is there anything I can help with, Doc? Towels? Water?"

"Coffee. I could use a cup." He pressed around on Lady's stomach, trying to get a feel for the pups. Lady lifted her head wearily and made an attempt to get up. "Good girl. Just relax." The Doc used a calming tone to keep Lady still.

"I'll go make the coffee and bring a tray of refreshments." Misty smiled and gave Bronson's hand a gentle squeeze. "When I'm nervous or stressed, I bake." She headed toward the kitchen.

Maybe it was all of the emotion and guilt over Lady, or his wary desire from time to time to settled down, but Bronson felt a soft spot for Misty boring into his heart. He admired Misty's strength and determination to make a new life in Crystal Cove. She'd overcome a tough upbringing on the road with her mother. Something happened to cause the two of them to part—for good. She could make a life here—maybe even a permanent job at Arlene's. He watched Doc with Lady, and glanced over to see Reese watching, so he decided to see if Misty could use some help in the kitchen.

"You got this, Doc? I'll go help Misty." It wasn't a question and he started out the room without waiting for an answer.

"Sure do," Doc called over his shoulder. "We have time."

In a few steps, Bronson stood at the kitchen entryway, watching Misty line up the coffee cups on a tray. She had the container of flour pulled out on the counter, along with sugar, milk, and eggs. Misty was in a baking mode.

He watched her move about the kitchen—his kitchen— like a natural, one who could easily fit perfectly into his life if he were thinking about a relationship—which he didn't need—but it would be nice…maybe. His mother had liked to bake a sour cream pound cake. He hadn't had it since she'd passed but the recipe was still in with the old cookbooks. He wanted to ask Misty if she could follow the recipe and make it exactly like his mother used to make.

"What are you doing?" he looked around the kitchen where there wasn't a recipe or cookbook in sight.

She had two round pans out with the insides covered with circles of parchment.

"Cake." She walked over to Bronson when he leaned on the counter.

The first chance he got, he'd go into the closet and pull out his mother's recipe. Then he would ask Misty if she would bake it as a surprise for his brothers. He smiled.

"Any special kind?"

She rested her elbows on the counter and looked him in the eyes. "Pound Cake," she said sweetly. "My grandmother's recipe." He didn't have the heart to ask her to make his mother's right then, and his hopes deflated as he decided to wait until another day to pull out her recipe. She moved back over to her mixer and he followed.

She was so confident and focused while she worked in the kitchen. Unlike him and his brothers who couldn't boil water. She hummed as she worked, and he decided to give her a little more help than she needed. He picked up an egg, a habit from when he was a kid, like he was going to crack it in the bowl.

"Have you come to help?" Misty looked over her shoulder at him with a smirk. He got the distinct impression she didn't believe he was there to cook, and she was right. He could make a bowl of cereal, but that didn't really count, but cracking the eggs had always been fun when he was a small boy. He put the egg back down.

"I'll just watch." He wanted to be close to her, and he didn't know why. It confused him. Feeling an unusual connection with Misty, a mixture of emotions about his mother cooking in the kitchen and poor Lady in the next room, was tripping all of his sensitivity chips. Something he wasn't used to. He was a man who didn't want or need a woman to complicate things in his life. Jim was a perfect example of how a man could lose his head when a woman was involved. Once that happened, your life wasn't your own.

She spoke while she worked. "I had to do something with my hands. I felt so helpless in there." Her cheeks flushed. She must have realized what she'd just said. Ignoring his amused gaze, she continued, "Once this is in the oven, I'll collect towels and make a warm basket for the pups." The coffeepot signaled the magical brew was finished. She stopped what she was doing, and with a shaky hand, filled the cups on the tray. "I have the jitters, and I didn't even try a sip yet." She brushed a few loosened curls off her forehead. They had escaped from the ribbon tied tightly in her hair. "Where're Radford and Braxton?" her pink full lips asked in a sweet voice.

Bronson frowned. "It's Friday." That meant, when the work at the ranch was finished for the day, his brothers took off with a couple of the workers. A few beers and a few women later, they would drive over to the local rodeo to ride and compete. It was the young and single crowd's weekend routine.

Normally Reese would be gone too, but like Bronson, Reese had an Achilles heel when it came to their animals. Growing up on a ranch, you tended to lose a dog or cat to unusual circumstances every now and then. Some people could accept it as part of life and move on. Bronson accepted it, but also learned from it. He tried to protect the animals he loved and himself from the painful loss. His mother had died when the boys were young, and his dad became an empty shell, so for a while, it was like losing both of his parents.

Eventually his father made his way back to the world of the living, but he was never the same. He never showed joy in the simple pleasures of life like he once had. Bronson used that as a learning experience. He wasn't about to let some woman ruin his life. Look how close he'd come with Delilah. She'd done him a favor by falling for someone else—saved him from himself and a life of hell with her. Not that he believed all women or marriage was bad—just bad for him.

And yet, he found himself here—in the kitchen—alone—with Misty—and he didn't know why, but he wanted to kiss her.

Misty picked up the tray of coffee, and he stepped in front of her. His eyes scanned her delicate features. "Here, let me carry it," he said, taking it from her hands. Their fingers touched, and he wanted his glide his hands all over her body.

From the next room, Doc Harrison yelled, "Here comes the first puppy."

After a long night of caring for the puppies, Misty returned home just before dawn and crawled into bed with the hope of catching a few hours of sleep before her alarm went off. At six thirty, she hit the snooze button, desperate to squeeze in five more minutes before she began the day by baking for Arlene's cafe.

The doorbell sounded followed by a loud knock at the front. Who could be on her front porch this early? Bright sunlight spilled in through the draperies, and she shielded her eyes. Rolling over to see what time it was, her bleary eyes burned. *Ten forty-five!* She'd overslept!

Flipping off the covers, she sprang out of bed, then threw on an old T-shirt and a pair of shorts before running out of the room. She almost slipped down the stairs on the way to the front door. A shadow moved by the small glass window embedded in the wood. Whoever it was knocked again. Loudly.

"Misty, are you all right?" a muffled woman's voice asked.

Arlene. She must have been worried. Why didn't she call first? Unlatching the door, she let the older woman inside. She looked like she'd been misted by a spray bottle or garden hose. Five minutes on the front porch in the morning heat and the humidity wilted anything that didn't contain chlorophyll in its DNA.

"Are you alone?" Arlene asked, looking around the room as if she was searching for a man who hid behind the living room draperies. She was dressed in capri shorts and a Lakeside Inn T-shirt. Her red hair looked like she'd just left a salon, a big contrast to Misty's stained clothing and no doubt sleep-filled eyes.

Misty glared at her. "Yes, I'm alone." She hadn't even had coffee yet. Grumpy and tired, she ground teeth annoyed. "I resent the question." She wasn't anything like her mother if that was what Arlene implied. She closed the door a litter harder than she'd wanted to. "I overslept." *There is such a thing as a phone.* Refraining from making the comment, she asked, "Is everything all right?"

She followed Arlene as she walked around the lower level of Misty's home, curious what Arlene was looking for. She was like a cat after a mouse stalking throughout the house.

"Would you like some coffee? I haven't had any yet." Her lips were dry and her throat parched from staying awake most of the night talking to Bronson, Reese, and Doc. They had helped Lady and watched her bond with her new puppies. What a shock it had been when they'd arrived. Such tiny little things for such a large dog. Doc Harrison said it looked like they were a mix from a much smaller breed. In a week or two, we would have a better idea what type of dog the father was. For a doctor who wasn't a vet, he'd done just fine, and later confessed he'd spent his residency years in a small community similar to Crystal Cove, where the doctor was also the vet.

"Sure, I'll have a cup." Arlene headed in the direction of the kitchen and sat down at the table. "So what happened? Are you sick?"

Misty's cheeks burned as Arlene studied her every move with a narrowed gaze. Could Arlene tell she was pregnant? She must look a sight with her messed up hair, worn out clothes, and red-rimmed eyes. Better to squelch any rumors before they started.

"The McCabe's dog, Lady, had a litter of puppies last night. I was up all night helping Lady get adjusted to being a new mother." She sighed. Who would help her get adjusted to being a new mother? Probably no one. Once they learned about her pregnancy, she doubted anyone in Crystal Cove would be there for her. Silence was golden—at least for now. She didn't have to answer any questions about who her baby's father was. By keeping it a secret there wasn't a chance anyone would bump into Beau and tell him. She didn't want to deal with Beau. The Rodeo circuit was large, but when it came to gossip, it was a small world. Anyone who followed the rodeo knew of Beau Carson. She grabbed two mugs out of the cabinet and started a pot of coffee. The smell of fresh-brewed coffee scented the air, and she couldn't wait to taste a sip.

Arlene's eyebrows shot up in surprise. "I didn't know they were breeding dogs." She stretched back in the chair and rested an elbow on the table.

"They didn't either. It was a surprise." A total shock actually, and even more confusing was how it happened. All dogs on the ranch were neutered. She doubted divine intervention. They'd figure it out one way or the other.

Arlene looked confused. "So you mean this wasn't a planned litter?"

"No." Misty took out the sugar and cream and placed it on the table, as she explained the story of the mix-up to

Arlene. "So it was a long night. I'm going over there later today, but with that many men living in the house, they can all take a puppy shift."

Arlene looked around the kitchen, and a few tears welled up in her eyes, one trickled down her cheek. "I haven't been inside this house since your grandmother passed. I was with her when she died." She pulled a tissue out of her brown leather purse and wiped her eyes.

Misty's lower lip began to tremble. "You were with her? Why didn't you tell me?" She fell into the chair across from Arlene and covered her face with her hands. The soft seat cushions comforted her body but not her heart. Arlene had been here, but she'd been playing waitress at the Wrong Way Diner.

"It's still very difficult to talk about. It's hard losing a lifelong friend, especially one as wonderful as Evelyn." Sadness blanketed her eyes, and she looked as if she were about to cry again.

"I…I'd assumed she died alone. Thank you, Arlene, for being here when my grandmother needed you." Conflicted emotions tore Misty apart. She was grateful Arlene was there for her grandmother, but angry and sad and disappointed that she'd missed seeing her alive one more time. Life could be cruel.

"Don't thank me. Your grandmother was there for me when I needed someone—anyone—the most in my life.

But that's for another time."

"Is that why you've helped me?" Her voice and hands were shaky, and she wavered on the edge of a sleep-deprived breakdown. The guilt compressed her chest so hard for a minute she couldn't breathe. She shouldn't have believed her mother's lies; the weight of regret crushed her already exhausted spirit. "Because you're friends with my grandmother?"

"Well, dear, yes and no. She loved you so very much. She'd neglected her health, but with what Evelyn had it didn't really matter." Arlene reached out and held Misty's hand. "There was nothing anyone could do. Your grandmother understood and never blamed you. That's all that matters."

Misty stood and retrieved the coffee pot. "Do you take cream and sugar?"

"Cream." Arlene leaned back so Misty could place the mug down on the table. Arlene had helped Misty whenever she could. Now she knew why. Her grandmother had helped Arlene in a time of need. She wondered how Arlene would feel when she learned about the baby.

"I can bake the pastries for today. I have time to do a few simple ones." Misty took the first sip of her coffee. "Mmm, just what I needed."

She could whip up an easy batch of cream puffs in about

an hour. Oh, and the Glazed Vanilla Gooey Bars. Those had been a favorite too. Éclairs and a few fruit pies could be baked in a little over an hour too. "I can bring them over early this afternoon."

Arlene raised her arm and waved her hand. "I know you're tired. If it's too much, take the day off. Heck it'll make people appreciate your baking all the more."

Maybe, but then she'd lose a day's wages too, and she needed every penny she could get right now. Levi hadn't given her an exact estimate on the repairs. Her intuition told her it must be high. Otherwise, he would have dropped it off already, wouldn't he? "I'll see how I feel after a shower." That should perk her up right after another cup of coffee.

Arlene set her cup down and leaned in. "Now, let's talk about your strategy to win that prize money." Misty saw the gleam in Arlene's eye. Obviously, she had something in mind to give her the competitive edge, but what? "Years ago your grandmother always came close but never won the competition outright. I want to see you win. I know you can do it. Not to insult your grandmother, but your flavors are more advanced than hers." She patted Misty's hand. "You're one special girl."

Arlene's compliment boosted Misty's confidence. She'd try to do her grandmother's memory proud. Winning this competition would jump-start the business to support her child. What better way to "test out" her recipe than at the workers' appreciation picnic. If all went in her favor, Misty would win and Crystal Cove would be the home of the new county champion.

As Misty pulled down the dirt road, she passed a field with numerous tractors parked in waist-high grass that needed a good mowing. From the looks of the old machines, they hadn't been started in years. The green grass was so tall you'd need a machete to cut a path to get to the equipment in the first place. Even worse, how would the machinery cut through the high grass once they were started? Several other types of old farm equipment were parked, or rather dumped, in random sections of the acreage.

Up ahead of her, she could see a portion of trimmed grass with a large house and a barn off to the right. A few goats and horses roamed around in a fenced in area surrounding the two buildings. At this distance, it looked like a typical country landscape painting. So peaceful—the beautiful

Florida flat land, with a large pond and cypress trees that shaded one half of the water where a few cows waded.

She knew Levi was home and she wanted to bring by this small cooler of meals before she went over to the 4M Ranch. The thought had occurred to her after her visit with Arlene this morning. She uncovered the reason Levi hadn't sampled anything she'd made for the Lakeside Inn. Arlene mentioned Levi never went out to eat after his wife died. Misty remembered Levi telling her Evelyn delivered meals to him when his wife passed away. It occurred to her this was a small community, and they were like a family to one another. Something she hadn't picked up on at first, but was beginning to get it.

When she came to the gate, she stepped out and opened it, careful not to let any of his four-legged friends escape. She pulled up and closed it behind her. As she approached, Levi walked out onto the front porch. He must have heard or seen her coming down the driveway.

She stopped the big diesel truck but didn't turn the engine off. Driving one of the McCabe's work trucks seemed like driving a bus to her, but she was thankful they let her use it. She hopped out, went around, and opened the side door where she pulled out the cooler of food.

Levi pushed his white cap back and called, "Hey, Misty. What brings you all the way out here?" He started down the front porch steps with a large old Labrador in tow. The aged chocolate companion let his tongue hang off to the side. The big baby looked like a large puppy who'd never grown up.

"I brought you a sample of my food and desserts," she called. "I figured you don't get out to often and you might like a night off from preparing meals."

A big grin slid across his face, and he reached out, eager to take the container she'd brought. Overjoyed, Misty's heart was warmed by his smile and tear-filled eyes. He was deeply touched over the gift of food.

"That's so kind of you, young lady. Thank you." He put one arm around her and gave her a squeeze. "You're just as sweet as your grandmother, and the picture of her when she was a young girl too.

Did she really look like her grandmother? Misty fought back tears that threatened to fall. "Don't thank me until you taste it. I hope you enjoy it."

"It smells delicious. I know I will. Don't think I forgot about your house. I'm working on a few things to help you out," he said. "I know Evelyn would want me to do the very best for her girl."

How lovely he was to care.

She'd never really thought of herself as Evelyn's girl. She liked the way it sounded, and it made her day to see his face lit up. As she climbed into the truck and waved good-bye, she realized Crystal Cove was beginning to feel like home.

She could relate to Levi. It was difficult being alone. She'd begun to make friends and extended family, but when it came right down to it, she was still all alone. Once the baby came, would Crystal Cove still welcome her with open arms? She didn't want to think about an answer now.

Bronson stood in the doorway of the large country kitchen, enjoying the sugary aroma of cinnamon spice that floated through the air. Something sweeter caught his attention: Misty's curves. The view from this angle looked good enough to eat, and he was in the mood for a little taste and not of what was baking in the oven.

The entire group of ranch hands scurried about in the final stages for tomorrow's picnic. Misty looked calm, fresh, and full of energy. The endless baking, chopping, and dicing of the massive amounts of food seemed to agree with her. He enjoyed how excited she was at the fact it would be consumed tomorrow by the families of the 4M Ranch. The volume of work didn't seem to faze her. His heart swelled with pride. This longtime family tradition had begun with his parents, and he was pleased

Misty seemed to enjoy it as much as he did.

Jim on the other hand, always had several meltdowns before it was all over. It was Jim's yearly ritual to cause a little drama when it came to the picnic. Clearly, the event was more than he was able to handle, and they all paid for it year after year. Bronson strode into the room.

"It sure does smell delicious in here."

Misty looked delicious too.

She moved with ease from the stove to the oven, making sure nothing burned. She turned and gave him a big smile. Her pink full lips, ripe and ready for a kiss—his kiss. He wanted their tenderness pressed against him. He wanted to kiss her in the worst way.

"Do you want a sample, cowboy?" she said, stirring the pot.

Boy, do I! Dressed in tiny pink shorts and a floral tank top that hugged her in all the right places, he wanted to wrap her in his arms and sample the sweet flavors she had to offer. He reached out and touched her shoulder.

"I have to admit I was skeptical you could handle this, but you proved me wrong." Rarely was he wrong about people, but this time he was. He didn't mind being mistaken when it came to Misty. Maybe he'd judged her too harshly. She seemed nothing like her mother. Misty was honest and genuine—traits he valued.

She turned to face him, her mouth inches from his. "People tend to misjudge. They only see what's on the surface instead of what's deep inside."

He wanted to get to know her better—what was inside. He ate her up with his eyes, then lost his fight, letting his mouth closed in on hers before either one of them could stop. She didn't protest. The kiss was sweet...tender... inviting, and she placed her arms about his neck in response. They held their embrace and savored the moment. She smelled so good, warm—sexy. She seemed surprised when he pulled himself away, but she didn't complain. She scanned his face as if looking for an answer. The passion he saw in her eyes stirred something in his groin.

Shocked by the adrenaline from the kiss, he mumbled, "I'm sorry. I don't know what came over me."

Liar! The room closed in, and he didn't care—he wanted more. He was sure she could hear the pounding of his heart echoing off the walls. She took a step back.

"Don't be." Her eyes pleaded in earnest. "I'm not."

He forced himself to release her from his grasp, not really wanting to let go. She smelled of sugar and vanilla with a splash of hot sauce from the food she was cooking. He could get used to this—a woman in his life. Someone soft and delicious—passionate.

He wasn't sorry at all. Bronson then leaned in and

planted another kiss, this time harder and more forceful, his mouth hungry for hers. He had things he wanted to tell her, but he let his lips do the talking. She gasped and let out a soft moan, eagerly accepting all he had to offer.

The gentle sound of paws entered the kitchen with the clop of heavy boots following right behind them.

"Lady and I came to see what's cooking," Radford said, taking in the scene. "Apparently, more than expected."

Startled, Bronson separated from Misty but kept a comfortable arm around her waist. His thumb stroked her soft skin, and he wanted to take her away from the 4M so they could be alone.

Radford gave Lady a gentle pat on the head, snatching an oatmeal cookie from a tray on the counter. Lady looked up at him in anticipation; she knew if they were in the kitchen, she would get a treat. He broke off a small piece and handed it to her before taking a bite.

"The puppies are doing great. Interesting combination border collie/poodle mix." Radford had an amused smirk on his face. The dark circles under his eyes gave away his tiredness. He'd had the night feeding shift for the pups. Someone had to make sure they were all fed equally. Poor Lady had been confused at first. Like any new mother, she'd needed time to adjust.

"Poodle?" Bronson and Misty said in unison. Lady barked, wanting another snack. Nursing mothers had to eat more often, and Lady was going to make sure they didn't forget it.

"Rad, tell me your joking. Who do we know with a poodle?"

Radford frowned and rolled his eyes toward the window where his two brothers could be seen standing on the patio talking to Levi.

"Levi doesn't have a poodle," Bronson snapped. Rad thought everything was a joke, but this was serious. They had to be responsible and find good forever homes for the puppies.

"Not Levi," Radford replied tartly. "Reese. He fessed up. He knows something about it." What did Rad mean by *something*? Reese either had information or he didn't.

Bronson pressed for more. "Like? I don't have time to play twenty questions. Spit it out."

"I think Reese should be the one to tell you." Rad paused. "In private." He looked at Misty when he said it, and Bronson understood his meaning loud and clear. It might be best if Misty didn't hear Reese's explanation. Surely, it involved Reese making a pit stop to flirting town, or whatever, and letting poor Lady run loose.

He turned to Misty. "I'll be right back." He removed his arm from around her waist then headed outside. What was Reese up to? Why couldn't he explain what had happened? Bronson didn't like chasing his baby brother around to get an answer, but that was Reese, slipping back into bad habits every once in a while, out having fun. He'd calmed down some since they were teenagers, but maybe he'd regressed and needed a firmer hand these days. Out of all of his brothers, Reese would be voted most likely to wind up in trouble—or cause trouble. He wasn't bad or anything, but he was a magnet for mischief. Often attracted and drawn to it, where jokes often went too far. His unappreciated sense of humor as a child triggered his parents to always appoint one of his brothers to watch out for him. After all these years, Bronson was still doing it.

From the kitchen window, Misty watched Bronson make his way outside to speak with his younger brother, puzzled why he'd left in such a hurry with the not-so-secret-message from Radford. She understood it was a private matter, but didn't understand what difference it made now. She shrugged and turned back to her work. There was still so much to do, and the picnic was less than a day away. Immediately after the event ended, she had to begin getting ready for the fair the following weekend. She tried to exhale and calm the anxiety building as she thought of her workload in the near future. Changing the subject of her thoughts, she turned to Radford to try to get a better understanding of the situation.

"So the puppies are half poodle. Why didn't Reese confess and tell Bronson himself?" she questioned Radford. "Why did Reese keep it a secret?" It didn't make any sense to her.

"You don't understand. There are a few things Bronson will not tolerate—things that will drive him away—shut him down and he won't forgive. One of them is lying and another one is deliberate deception.

"Reese is a big chicken. When we discovered Lady was going to be a mother, he should have come forward. I think Bronson wouldn't feel like he does now—betrayed —but he tends to overreact." He moved closer to Misty. "It's because of Delilah." Radford shook his head and shrugged. "We kinda suspected she was cheating but didn't have any proof. So we kept it to ourselves. At first, Bronson held us responsible for making him look foolish to the townsfolk. He was hurt and embarrassed. Afterward, he realized even if we had told him, he'd have never believed us. Delilah was very persuasive, and he was under her spell."

"Some women have that type of power over a man." Not that she ever had or wanted it, but some women could manipulate and fog up a man's head. Love had a way of doing that to people; that was why Misty stayed clear of love.

Then a thought struck her and guilt nearly swallowed Misty as if she were struggling in quicksand up to her neck. She began to cough, placing a hand to her throat, trying to release the imaginary pressure. The anxiety from the responsibilities over the next few days were growing. Now, she had the sinking feeling of remorse for her deception to add to the load, but she wasn't ready to tell Bronson or anyone about the baby. When all the excitement died down, and if things progressed further in their relationship, she would tell him. After all, it was just a kiss. One kiss—nothing more.

Radford joked, "I better go smooth things over, before it comes to blows."   He grabbed his hat from a nearby chair and went out to join Bronson. Misty watched him through the window. Both Bronson and Reese turned to look at Radford, but before he could make it over to them, Reese stormed off.

Outside, it took Bronson and his two brothers, a group of hands, and the ranch foreman to direct the delivery of the tents, tables, and chairs. The supply truck had arrived early that morning to unload the rented lounge chairs and umbrellas to accommodate the crowd of people invited to this year's event. It was taking all day to get things ready. Levi helped where he could, pitching in; they appreciated his help. With a live band setting up under a poolside cabana, the added furniture would allow a day of fun at the pool.

Misty's smoker had been moved to the 4M along with several others, some grills, and a few food trucks. The McCabes borrowed from their neighbors. Each year they showed their appreciation with a huge celebration for the ranch hands and their families, and they always included their extended families living in Crystal Cove. The McCabe brothers were generous, following the tradition their parents had begun so long ago. Misty suspected it was a way to honor their parents too.

Misty wrestled with all the excitement. This event would be the preliminary test before the fair. If the ranchers and their wives gave her positive reviews for her barbecue sauce and the meats she cooked, she would be in business. The beef brisket, ribs, pulled pork, and chicken had to be the best in the state. It was a large order, but she would do her best to rise to the challenge. Everything she owned rode on it, and more importantly, so did her baby's future. She imagined her barbecue sauce bottled, labeled, and marketed on every grocery store shelf. Well, maybe she was getting a bit ahead of herself. She'd take one step at a time.

A dull ache in her lower back reminded her she'd been on her feet far too long. She gently rubbed her stomach. She wasn't showing yet, but her baby was there. Taking a small break, she walked over by the window. Outside,

Bronson barked out a few orders to several hands. Looking at his handsome face, she began to daydream about her baby. Would it be a boy or a girl? Would her child look like Beau or take after her? Would her little boy want to ride the rodeo like Bronson and his brothers?

Bronson?

She snapped out of her quiet fantasy. Where the heck had that come from? Beau was a rodeo champion. Beau was her baby's father *not* Bronson. Just because she cooked for the McCabes didn't mean they wanted her to become their cook permanently. Jim would be back, and when he returned, she'd be forced to move on. She didn't mind finding different employment, and if she was lucky enough to win the grand prize at the fair, then she'd be able to bottle her barbecue sauce and sell it locally. Who knows, if she was fortunate and business was good, she could even sell it online. She'd only need a computer and internet. Other people had started that way, why shouldn't she?

Even landing one or two corporate accounts would be the answer to her prayers. She'd be able to support both herself and the baby. She had so much work ahead of her, but for now, she'd focus on getting through the picnic tomorrow.

With her mind in a fog, she heard the door open. Radford walked back in and poured himself a glass of water. He grabbed a paper towel from the roll and wiped his brow.

"Sure is hot out there." Resting a hip on the counter, he picked up his glass had drank another sip.

"I'll say," she murmured. Feeling his eyes on her, she shifted uncomfortably in her chair, trying to shake off his gaze.

Radford remained silent, watching Bronson through the window. "You two would make a great couple," he said as if he'd been assessing her from afar.

"I'm not looking for a relationship and neither is Bronson." She lied through her smiling teeth. It wasn't that she wasn't looking for a relationship, rather she longed for a family. A family she never really had growing up. Was it wrong to want a home and someone to love? She had the house, and even if it needed repairs, it was hers free and clear. She was very blessed her grandmother had left it to her. Her heart ached with the knowledge that her grandmother was the only person in her life who'd loved her.

Now, a precious baby on the way would enrich her life and who knew what the future would bring. She needed to talk to Carly—bad. She missed her best friend, and the daily girl-to-girl chats while they worked side by side. What was Carly up to these days? Misty studied Bronson's large broad shoulders and muscular arms as he lifted supplies off the truck. He wasn't afraid to get his hands dirty or pitch in to get the job done. Some ranch owners would never step in to help. They'd order hands to do all the dirty work. Behind her, she heard the lid of the roasting pan open. When she turned around, she saw Radford filling up a sample plate from the food she'd prepared. He'd piled the dish high by the time he came over to the table.

Radford sank his teeth into the roll filled with barbecued pork. "Mmm, delicious."

"Take human bites," she joked. "Why are you having a sandwich now?"

If the four brothers feasted on her food all day today, they were sure to make a huge dent in the supply for tomorrow's picnic. The endless pans and cleanup had her worn out already.

He furrowed his brow. "Why not? I'm hungry." He looked at her as if she were wearing two heads and continued eating.

She grabbed a paper napkin from the holder and pushed it in front of him while she scolded, "You do realize I have been working on this for days, and if you and your brothers think you're going to start the party early, you can think again."

Rad stopped eating, his gaze locked with hers. "Where'd that come from?" He chuckled. "But you're right. I'm sorry." Then he smiled. "You're gonna fit in here just fine."

She didn't know where her temper flare-up had come from either. What did he mean by "fit in?" The town, at the ranch, or in Bronson's life?

M isty watched the sun peek over the horizon to fill the sky with mauve and gold while she sipped a cup of steaming hot coffee. She closed her eyes and enjoyed the freshly brewed fragrance that floated out of the white ceramic mug. It went down easy, and she finished the last drop, allowing it begin to work its magic. Still tired from yesterday, she'd need a second cup to get her body in gear to start the day, but she lacked the energy to get up from the comfortable porch swing.

Yesterday had been hectic and unusual with the four brothers on edge with each other. When Bronson returned inside from his talk with Reese, he didn't say much. Rather than tippy-toe around Bronson in silence, she'd decided to go home. She didn't have time to figure out what was going on between the brothers; she had more on her plate than she could handle.

The porch creaked whenever the wooden swing swayed, and she imagined mornings in the not-so-near-future, holding her baby, rocking her little bundle to sleep. She hadn't been around babies much at all. There was an awful lot to learn, and she didn't have a clue where to begin.

By this time next week, she would be able to see her baby for the first time with an ultrasound. The days couldn't go by fast enough till her next doctor's appointment. She raked her fingers though her hair and massaged her scalp. Her head ached from the excitement and stress over the past few days. Such a wild mixture of emotions spun around inside of her. Joy swelled in her heart at the thought of the precious life she carried, but with it came a sadness that she was virtually alone with no one to share it with. She stilled the swing with her left foot and hoisted herself up, mindful of every ache from standing all day on the tile floors at the ranch. Hours of food prep had taken their toll and her back and feet had paid the price. She opened the door, making her way to the kitchen where she poured a second cup. Today she was going to push the doctor's limit. On second thought, she'd only drink a few more sips and dump the rest in the sink.

Her cell phone rang. Who could be calling at this time in the morning? The screen glowed the name *Carly*. Guilt made her itch like an old wool sweater. They hadn't spoken since Misty arrived in Crystal Cove. For a few days, she hadn't had the money to keep her cell phone on, but then she'd been so preoccupied with making a life in the quaint little town and Bronson that she'd kinda left the friendship hanging. She should have made more of an effort to keep in touch. She hit the answer button, eager to fill her in on the recent details of her life.

"Hey, girl, what's happening?" Why would Carly be calling before the sun rose in Texas? Had she even gone to bed yet? "You've been on my mind." *It wasn't a lie really.*

Carly was the closest thing she had to a sister. They'd shared everything before Misty high-tailed it back to Crystal Cove. The fact that she'd never found the right time to contact Carly made her realize she wasn't being honest with herself about the loss of her grandmother. What else wasn't she being honest about? Plenty!

"Misty, I've finally reached you. You don't know how many times I've tried." The panic-stricken voice sounded desperate through the cell phone. "I've been worried sick about you." They'd played phone tag a few times, leaving messages, but Carly never had sounded this desperate or even concerned by the brief "Call me" voicemails she'd left. This didn't sound like her.

"Is everything all right?" Misty couldn't understand what could have brought on this much anxiety. It wasn't like Carly didn't know where Misty had been. While waiting for her reply there was a large crackling in the phone. She couldn't make out what Carly was saying.

"What did you say?"

The static in the connection stopped just as Carly repeated, "I'm at the bus station."

"What bus station? Where?"

"I'll be there in two days. Can you meet me?" A bus roared and the sound of street traffic in the background drowned her out for the second time.

"Of course," Misty replied automatically, raising her voice to be heard over the noise. "What's going on?" Carly coming here—to Crystal Cove? "For how long?" So many questions tumbled through her mind, but she fired off the biggest ones, hoping to get some answers.

Carly was self-sufficient, carefree, and lucky enough to have a large family. Not one of them lived close to her, but she kept in touch with them on a regular basis. They were scattered about Texas, and even though it was a huge state, every few months she'd take a weekend to visit them. Misty had never envied anyone, but she'd struggled on those long weekends alone, wishing to belong to a family of her own.

"I need a change of scenery is all. Life in this town is boring without you." She didn't blame Carly for wanting to leave the tourist trap town they'd lived in. It seemed like worlds away from the life Misty was living now. Something about Crystal Cove touched her heart. The town was beautiful but the people even more so.

"I have so much to tell you." Misty wanted to fill Carly in on the blow-by-blow details since she'd arrived to Crystal Cove—her grandmother's death, Bronson, the fair—but the poor connection made it impossible to explain.

"I want to hear it all, but we're starting to board the bus," Carly yelled over the blaring loudspeaker in the background. "I've gotta go." A roar and the hiss of hydraulic brakes echoed through the phone.

"Call me later tonight if you can," Misty hollered back, hoping Carly could hear her.

"Will do."

Then the line went dead.

Misty frowned. Could Carly be in some sort of trouble?

In the deafening silence, she heard a truck pull into the driveway. Now what? The shuffle of boots on the porch and the gentle rap at the front door followed a few seconds later. She set her cup down and hurried to answer it.

"Who is it?" She wasn't expecting anyone—not this early. Unless it was Levi dropping off her estimate for the repairs. Maybe he had a job in town and was starting at the crack of dawn.

"Bronson," he announced. The sound of his voice sent a thrill throughout her body. Heat rose to her cheeks. She opened the door, realizing she wore a faded oversized T-shirt for pajamas. Her eyes locked on his in an oh-so-glad-to-see-you moment. A wicked, lopsided grin on his unshaven face made him look sexy and a little dangerous. How she wanted to believe he was here because he wanted her. There had to be another reason. She stood there, studying his chiseled features while several mockingbirds serenaded them in the background.

"Mind if I come in?"

Her stomach rolled over with anticipation. Should she let him in? Why was he here? She opened the door farther and stepped aside to allow him to enter. Her cheeks burned as he raked his eyes over her flimsy T-shirt.

"Did I wake you?"

"No, I've been up for a while. I couldn't sleep. Too much going on in my head." Like the baby, the picnic, the fair, and now add Carly to the mix. She shut the door behind him and said, "Coffee?" She needed desperately to finish that second cup. He took off his hat, dropped it on a table by the door and nodded. The rumpled hair, the scent of alpha male, and his unshaven jaw made him look incredibly sexy. Her pulse kicked up a few beats. She wanted to run her fingers through his tousled hair.

He followed close, and her body reacted. Shallow breaths

caught in her chest while they made their way into the kitchen. She glanced at the counter. Her eyes widened when she spotted the bottle of prenatal vitamins in plain view. *Damn.* She swept them up with her left hand, opened the cabinet with the other, and shoved them inside, then quickly pulled out another mug. She blew out a long breath. She wasn't ready to have that conversation with anyone yet. Except Carly. Maybe Carly's impromptu arrival would be a good thing after all.

After filling his cup with coffee, she turned around to hand it to him. Something sizzled when his fingers brushed against hers. He paused, tilted his head, and arched an eyebrow, giving her a long, burning look. Did he feel it too or was it her imagination?

She stammered. "W-what brings you here this early?"

The workers' appreciation picnic was in a few hours. They both had so much work to do before then; he should be back at the ranch. If she didn't get a move on, time would get away from her and she'd be late.

Bronson took a few steps closer. He raised the mug to his lips and blew a puff of steam from the brew before he continued.

"I had a phone call late last night from Jim," he hesitated. "He's coming back in a few days with his…" He groped around for the word and spat out, "Wife." His face contorted so it looked almost painful as he forced out the last word. The look in his eyes said, *"I'm sorry."*

She sucked in air as if a fist had punched her right in the gut. She'd known Jim would return...eventually, and he had been gone a long time before she'd even arrived in town.

He shrugged. "I wanted you to hear it from me." He reached out and brushed away a few wisps of hair from her cheek. She closed her eyes. His touch softened the blow of the news, and she wanted to believe Bronson cared for her—more than as an employer. They had a bargain, nothing more—but what if it wasn't—what if he felt it too? Better not raise her hopes with fantasies.

"I understood from the beginning the job wasn't permanent. It was a temporary position until Jim returned."

His voice filled with sympathy. "Don't worry. This isn't going to affect our bargain." The bargain was only the half of it. The job of cook paid well, and she could use those funds to help repair her grandmother's car or the roof or buy baby furniture. Now she had to work harder and manage a strict budget until she could find another job. In her situation, one job wouldn't cut it against all of her mounting expenses.

Misty struggled to hide her disappointment. Crushed because she would lose being part of a family—his family—even if it had only been for a few weeks as their cook. For the first time in years, it felt like she belonged. It was nice to be included and be cared for. She understood it had to end whether or not Jim returned, but she had wanted this fantasy to last a little while longer. She made a cup of herbal tea to calm her nerves, rather than finish the second cup of coffee she'd poured earlier.

She cleared her throat. "Don't give it another thought." A few tears pooled, causing her vision to blur. She looked to the left in an effort to hide her emotion. Reaching for her cup, she took a sip of tea, allowing the steaming liquid to seep throughout her body and warm her bruised spirit.

"I have so much to do to get ready for the fair anyway. I appreciate all you've done for me." Her lower lip betrayed her with a quiver, and she tried to hide the sadness from her voice. "How are the puppies?" She tried switching the subject to lighten the mood and her spirits.

The tiny fur balls were hard to resist. What was a happy subject for her was still a thorn in Bronson's side by the grimace he wore.

"Something wrong?" The question came out a little shaper than she'd intended.

"No. Not really. Unless you call falling in love with the entire litter wrong." Mr. Strong Badass was a softy when it came to family. Lady and now her puppies were a part of his family. The little black and white balls of cuteness would cast a spell on anyone who laid their eyes on them.

He ran his fingers through his thick hair. "I don't see how I can find good homes for all of them." A warm glow streaked through the window, illuminating Bronson's face as the sun rose higher in the sky. As he looked up, the kindness in his eyes made her heart melt.

"You will. You'd be surprised how a new puppy can wiggle its way into someone's heart in a matter of seconds."

"No, that's not true," he murmured.

Really? His biggest worry this morning was finding homes for a few puppies, and the return of Jim, while she had to find a way to supplement her income, repair a home, and prepare for a baby. Then there was the state fair and creating a strategy to win the prize money she desperately needed. All of which created a mild state of panic to jump-start her day.

"What isn't true?" She didn't understand, and while she waited for an answer, she memorized his chiseled features, once again irritated by the Jim situation.

"Something's wrong." His gaze intensified, so she braced herself for what was about to come next, holding her breath until he spoke. "I don't want Jim to return. What I mean is, when Jim left, I was shocked, and believe me, we were eating some god-awful cooking because of it too." He pushed back the chair and stood up. "All I could think about was how he could do this to us and when will he come back. Now that he is, I'm angry. He up and left us, and now he says he's heading back to Crystal Cove—married—and I'm supposed to be relieved...happy...just pick up where we left off?" He clenched his fists, walked over to the window, and gazed out.

Staring at his broad shoulders from behind, she didn't know what to say or how to respond to his conflicted emotions. From what he told her, Jim practically raised them and devoted his life to the McCabe family. He deserved to make a life for himself now that they were grown men. In some ways, they were being selfish, but she chose her words carefully.

"Do you think of Jim as family...employee...both? Your reaction to him will dictate your relationship from this point forward when he arrives."

She moved closer behind him. This was a conversation for another time, not one to have with the picnic about to start in a few hours. But she couldn't turn Bronson away, not now, not when he needed her. The longer he stayed, the further behind her prep work slipped. He'd supported her when she'd first stepped foot in Crystal Cove, but their deal was about to be over. After today, he didn't owe her a thing, but she would owe him for the supplies until after the state fair. She'd fulfilled her obligation, and the first part of their deal was complete. Then she'd focus all her attention on the fair and how to win the prize money. Her grandmother's barbecue sauce recipe had to wow the judges and the public, not just a few Crystal Cove residents.

He blew out a long breath. "When my mother died, Jim was there to help my dad and keep things going—keep us going as a family. Just when we thought we survived the worst and had established some sort of a routine, my father died. My brothers, the ranch, and our workers became my responsibility. Jim stepped in as a father figure. Now he has have wife. A woman we know nothing about." He spun around, leaving mere inches between them.

She tilted her head upward to meet his gaze. Warmth bloomed in her chest. He was close—too close for comfort—and she wanted to feel his arms close around her, the warmth of his lips crushing down on hers. Instead, he raised his hand, and with his thumb, brushed her cheek. Then he leaned down and did what her body yearned for him to do—place a kiss upon her lips. At first, it was soft and gentle, then firmer…and intoxicating. The room swayed, and she wanted to fall into his arms and stay there forever. The way he kissed her said he felt it too.

Would he want to start a life with a family? Would he be willing to accept her baby? She pressed harder into him, and he parted her lips with his tongue.

"Misty," he murmured in a husky voice. His unshaven cheeks abraded her skin, and his lips trailed down her neck. "It's been so long since…" he whispered against her flesh.

"Bronson, I…" She wanted this, but it wasn't right. Not here. Not now. She didn't want to be his temporary comfort.

She wasn't experienced. Sure, she'd had a few flirtatious romances, but never a relationship to show for it. Was Bronson offering her something more? Did he want a romantic tryst or the real relationship she longed for?

She should stop this before it went any further. She didn't need to complicate her life any more than it already was. He was emotionally confused, and she didn't want to be a comforting release and end up emotionally drained and regretting what happened. She'd lived that moment already in her life and it didn't need repeating. The night with Beau had resulted in a child, but getting too close to Bronson could only result in heartbreak.

"Bronson, we can't, it…wouldn't be right." She pressed her hands against his chest to stop his progress, but her head screamed, "*Don't stop.*"

She groped for excuses, blurting out the first things that came to mind. "I have a lot of work to do. I have a visitor from San Antonio arriving in a few days." She had to get a hold of the situation or lose her heart for good.

Large blue eyes framed by thick brown lashes peered up at him with desire.

A visitor? Did Misty have a man? A past relationship on his way into town?

His heart balled up like a crumpled piece of paper then flattened as if it had been stomped on. The words doused his body like a bucket of ice water and twisted his hormones back into reality. The fantasy of whisking her off to the bedroom flew right out the window.

What the hell had he been thinking? Shouldn't he at least find out who was visiting before he lost himself and his heart to a woman who may belong to another? His throat clenched, and the dryness in his mouth made him lick his lips. His primitive attraction made it hard for him to concentrate. She'd never mentioned anyone, male or female, the entire time she was with him at the ranch. In fact, she led him to believe she'd been totally alone for the last few years. Now, she had a visitor?

He held her in his arms and gave a gentle squeeze, determined to force Misty to answer him. "A friend?" Sarcasm punctuated each word. Her eyebrows knit together as though sensing his mood shift, and a frown marred her lips.

She scanned his face. "Yes. Carly. We worked together at the diner back in San Antonio." Her smile grew wide and his heart quivered with beats of excitement as relief coursed through him at her answer. But why should he be relieved? He had no plans for a woman in his life. He had all the responsibility he could handle between his brothers and the ranch. This closeness was dangerous. She smelled so sweet and sexy. Like cinnamon and sugar. He wanted one more taste of her delicate, tender lips but resisted the urge. Shallow breaths kicked up his pulse, but he tamped it down.

"We've played phone tag a few times. I've been so busy with everything here. I'm embarrassed I haven't tried harder to get in touch with her."

"I'd say you've had more than your share to deal with." He relaxed his hold on her arms, letting his fingertips linger. The heat of the moment dissipated as his clarity returned, but the realization Misty had begun to carve a place in his heart became all too real.

He'd better get out of there before the situation worsened. He was about to make an excuse to leave when the doorbell rang. Simultaneously, their heads snapped toward the front door.

Misty turned away from him. "Now, who can that be?"

Bronson followed close behind her as she left the room. She opened the door a crack, just to peek.

"Arlene. What brings you here this early?" She opened the door a bit wider.

She looked disheveled, with a cigarette behind one ear and her red hair teased and spiked-up so it reminded him of a bird's nest. Arlene looked at Misty then right past her to pierce Bronson with a stare, then she cleared her throat.

"Seems like I've come at a bad time. I thought you could use a hand with the preparations for the picnic, but I see you already have two strong ones." She smirked.

Misty snapped, "It's not what you think," before peering at Bronson over her shoulder.

"What makes you think I'm thinking anything?" Arlene quipped. She stood firm in her position at the doorway, waiting for Misty to invite her in. The awkward silence of the moment hung in the air.

Damn, this will be spread all around Crystal Cove. Time to exit.

Bronson placed his hat on his head and nodded toward the woman. "Arlene, nice to see you. I was just leaving."

Misty opened the door and stepped aside to allow him to pass.

"I bet you were." Arlene winked with a sly chuckle. "Misty, can I come in?" Arlene was on a mission this morning, and Bronson couldn't wait to escape her scrutiny.

"Sure." Misty motioned Arlene inside.

He maneuvered around Arlene, desperate make his way out of the uncomfortable situation, and blew out a long breath. He was about to be grilled today more than the meat at the picnic. Suddenly the adrenaline rush of today's barbecue turned to dread.

Debra Fisk

The drive home seemed longer than usual, and Bronson was more aggravated than a horse with a burr under the saddle. Aggravated with himself for the emotions confusing his brain when it came to Misty. Why had he rushed over there? He had used the excuse of Jim, but the truth was it could have waited until Misty showed up to cook later today. A knot twisted in his gut. He wanted to see her and spend time with her. Which was ridiculous because there was no chance in a future for the two of them. He snorted at his foolishness.

When he was away from her, as he was now, his head began to clear and he remembered the reasons why he never wanted a wife or family of his own. He didn't need or want another ounce of responsibility. He'd received his share of it at an early age, managing the ranch and taking care of his brothers. He'd been living a life full of responsibility ever since. His father's death had forced him to grow up before he was ready, and sometimes, he resented it...life...the hand it dealt him, but at the same time, he was grateful for all the support he had. Look at Misty; she'd received a shitty hand from the happy deck of life, and yet, she wasn't bitter, angry, or jealous of others.

Ever since Delilah had dished him a double whammy, schooling him in a lesson on life and love, he'd stayed focused on his responsibilities, ignoring women for the most part. Avoiding any real relationships and just satisfying his physical needs now and then. He planned to survive years, maybe the rest of his life, like that, and then the first woman he felt a real attraction for was the product of a wayward mother. What could Misty possibly know about a stable relationship? He'd shouldered the weight of the ranch and his brothers all these years and he wasn't going to add another ounce of responsibility to his back. Hell, Reese still needed to be managed, and Bronson wasn't going to add a wife and kids—ever—to his list of things to do for the day. Yet the Eagle Scout in him tugged at his heart, reaching out and wanting to help her. He assumed she desired what most women did: marriage, children—a family deal.

He had to face facts. He wasn't in the market for adding to his family. He had all he could take care of. Kids took over your life, making constant demands, and women were needy. He'd observed the ranch hands and how their families consumed them. He wanted none of that. Not ever. The near slip when he looked into Misty's eyes made him realize he'd better keep his distance. He couldn't afford not to. Too much was at stake—his future and his peace of mind. Life was good just as it was. He didn't like change—change was bad. Every experience he'd had with change had caused his life to spin out of control, and it took all of the strength he'd had to right it.

After his mother passed away, it took them a few years to reach a degree of family normalcy. Then the unexpected death of his father left him in charge of everything. With Jim by his side for support, he'd managed to take control of his brothers and the ranch. Determined to prove he could handle responsibility, he'd increased profits and held their fragile family together. The ranch thrived more today than it had in years. He sighed. At least *that* was an accomplishment.

Bronson slowed his truck to a crawl as he pulled up to the home he loved more than life itself. This was where his heart lay. The memories of the generations of his family before him rested on this very ground. He sat and stared at the McCabe history before him, feeling content. Lush green pastures, fine herds of cattle, areas of citrus groves with decades of blood, sweat, and tears buried in the soil.

Radford opened the front door, stepped outside, and leaned against the porch railing. Confusion marred his face, and Bronson wasn't interested in explaining why he'd gone to Misty's before dawn. Rad was down the steps and almost to the truck by the time Bronson reached for the handle and opened the door, but before he could say a word, Rad pounced on him with the expected ball of questions.

"Is something wrong? Where the heck had you been? What time did you leave?" Rad was so close Bronson could feel Rad's breath move the hair on the nape of his neck as he threw out the questions.

"Early," he said, answering only the last question.

With the palm of his hand, he flung the door closed and made his way slowly up the few steps to the porch. He paused long enough to look his brother in the eye—easy to do since the two were almost twins in height. Rad waited in silence but Bronson didn't have to explain his actions to Rad. He brushed by Radford and went inside. The morning quiet left nothing but the tick of the wall clock and his thoughts rattling around in his brain. The door opened and closed behind him. Rad didn't say a word as he moved around to look at Bronson dead on.

Pouring himself a cup of coffee, Bronson said, "I went to see Misty." One bad thing about living with your brothers was someone was always around sticking their nose in your business.

Rad lifted his eyebrows. "And?" Determined to get more

answers, he blocked Bronson's path. Rad raked his fingers though his hair, smoothing the rumpled mass.

"And nothing. I went to tell her about Jim." Flimsy, but he'd talked himself into it at some point in the middle of the night. He'd wanted to gaze into her big blue eyes, touch her soft skin, and smell the sweet scent of her hair.

"What are you doing, man?" Rad looked at him with disbelief.

Good question. What was he doing? Why did Misty flip his world inside out in a way that seemed natural—easy and carefree. Something about her was different from other women he'd known. He tried to put his finger on it. Their relationship was—comfortable—that was how he felt when he was around her. For the first time in years, he had a heightened sense of happiness touch him inside. How could he explain that to Rad without sounding foolish or sappy, and yet, at the same time, he knew it was temporary. This fun, flirtatious thing with her had to end before it went further.

"She's had a tough past. I'm not heartless." Another excuse to avoid what was really going on inside of him. The connection to Misty deepened even with his resistance.

Radford eyed him suspiciously. "Hey, I didn't say you were. It's just—" He shook his head. "Never mind."

It wasn't like Bronson to act on impulse, but with Misty,

every bit of rationality flew out the window. After today and the picnic, getting his head on straight would be his number one priority.

"I thought I heard voices down here. What's going on?" Reese entered the room in his scruffy brown slippers and two puppies fast on his heels. "Is Misty here to make breakfast yet?" He staggered over to the coffee pot and poured himself a cup.

Bronson snapped, "No. And you better get used to the idea that she's leaving. As soon as Jim returns, she won't be cooking us breakfast or anything else. After today, our deal is over and she's moving on. She has the state fair to win and a life to lead." He walked over to the table, pulled out a chair, sat down, and stared out the window. The beauty of the morning sun glimmering on the dewy leaves gave no hint to the scorching temperatures of the day's highs.

"Did I miss something?"

"Jim called. He's coming back. End of story," Radford stated bluntly. "To tell the truth, I'm glad things are going back to the way they were. Nothing against Misty, but, Bronson, you've been different. Besides, this is a man's home, and as much as we love to spend time with the ladies, this is our place and they have theirs—you know what I mean."

"Agreed," the three of them said in unison.

Bronson's next sip of coffee went down like liquid chalk. Though his gut said he had to do it, the thought of a life without Misty in it sickened him

Misty turned to face Arlene. "I expect you to keep your mouth shut. I don't want people getting the wrong idea," she warned Arlene with an arched eyebrow. She turned and walked back into the kitchen. "I mean it." She made her tone sharp to be a firm warning that she meant business. Every town had a local gossip, and Arlene was Crystal Cove's.

The wrinkled woman followed on her heels. "I'm insulted you have such a low opinion of me. Besides, who would I tell?"

Low opinion?

"Try anyone you bumped into. Anyway, Bronson came over this morning to let me go—so to speak. Jim will be back in a few days to claim his old position." A sour taste filed her mouth as the words rolled off her tongue. She had no right to feel this way. They had a business deal; nothing more. She shouldn't have blurred the lines or allowed her emotions to get involved, creating a fantasy where she was part of the McCabe family. Her life would return to normal now that the deal was done. Time to shift her focus to the cash prize awaiting her.

The past few weeks, she'd been existing day to day. She desperately needed to take charge of the situation and repair her home with a plan to support her baby. Her grandmother's recipe had come so close to winning in the past, but now she was sure, with her few tweaks, the recipe would be a winner.

"It's for the best. You can do much better making specials for my place and selling them on your own. Before long you'll be making twice as much as he paid you." Arlene pressed her lips into a flat sly smile.

Misty loved Arlene's optimism. If Arlene was right, her money troubles would be over, but winning the prize money was vital to her long-term plan. She needed to shift all of her focus on mixing something unique—a surprise ingredient—into her entrees. Yes, that was the way she would win. The sooner she put distance between Bronson and her life the better.

"I want to get through this day and be done with it. I need to move on with my life, away from the McCabe brothers. It's been fun, but I have to live in the real world —mine not theirs." Her heart clenched at her foolish fantasy. The three of them could never be a family— Bronson, her, and the baby. What man would want another man's child? If he was attracted to her, it was out of some damsel in distress syndrome—not love or desire.

"You know, I've been thinking. Way back when your grandmother entered the fair, she came so close to taking home the prize money. The recipe you've created from hers is even better. There's no way it's not going to win first place." Arlene tilted her head with an assuring smile.

Misty swore she could see Arlene's pupils light up with dollar signs. "What are you thinking?"

Arlene had a head for business; anyone who could turn a profit in this small town with limited resources had to be a shrewd businesswoman—or doing something illegal. Misty turned around, pulled out a chair, then landed firmly in the seat, ready to hang on Arlene's every word.

Arlene paced back and forth in the kitchen. Head down with her hands behind her back, she spent several moments deep in thought before starting to speak. Then she spun around on her heels and snapped her fingers. "We need to gather a support team to help the day of the fair." Throwing her head back, she chuckled. "That's exactly what we need. I'm brilliant." She charged toward Misty, grabbing her by the arms and gave them a squeeze. "There's going to be thousands of people there, day and night."

Well, yeah, but what was her point? Misty tried to follow where Arlene was going with this line of thinking but got lost. A support team—how? Making plates of food?

Working the sales line? She would need a few extra hands to help, but a support team sounded like a lot more than she was bargaining for. After all, they would have to expect some form of payment. Right? And she had limited funds.

"With a support team to drive the business to *your* booth." Arlene's eyes nearly bugged out of her head. "Your barbecue is bound to capture the attention of the crowd and judges." She released Misty's arms, allowing the blood to pulsate back into her muscles. Misty gently rubbed the spots where Arlene had stopped the circulation, positive she'd have bruises by tomorrow from Arlene's death grip. Her hands tingled from the rush of blood running back into her fingertips.

"I'm not understanding how this support team is going to *drive* people to my booth." It seemed like a good idea, but how could they channel the crowd her way? She didn't have a winning reputation like other contestants or an advertising budget to market her sauce. Heck, she hadn't even thought of a name for it yet. She rolled around a few ideas in her head.

Misty's Barbecue?

Barbecue Mist?

Southern Sauce?

"There's so much to think about. Deciding on a name for it too."

"That's easy." Arlene rolled her eyes. "When I walked in and saw the way Bronson looked at you—the fire in his eyes was intense. I'd say he had *Summer Heat*." Arlene paused for a second, looking at Misty, waiting for some kind of reaction, then continued to mull over the possibilities for marketing, repeating different brand names and slogans to go with Summer Heat.

"Summer Heat," Misty repeated. It could work.

"Well?" Arlene arched an eyebrow at Misty's silence.

"Well what?"

"What do you think of Summer Heat?"

"Oh, I like it. Very creative." Misty's thoughts began to spin with ideas, bouncing off the head start Arlene had given her.

"Your last name reminds me of the sweet refreshing flavors of summer balanced with a twisted blend of heat." She licked her index finger and swiped it in the air before making a sizzling sound.

"Summer Heat," Misty repeated slowly, letting the words roll off her tongue. "It's perfect." She could visualize the label, logo, and a sampler pack needed to get her product off the ground. Now, for the hard part: winning the prize money. She bit her lip in thought—back to the support team. Whom could she ask to be on her team? Who in town would be willing to help?

"I know I can get the girls: Darla and Audrey. Then there's Levi. I'm sure Bronson and his brothers will agree to help and—"

"Wait. Hold on. I'm not sure I want to involve Bronson or any of the McCabes for that matter. We both just agreed a few seconds ago that I needed to take charge of my life—move away from the dependency of the McCabe brothers and branch out on my own." She hated the way her voice rose a few octaves when she was stressed. "I like the concept of the support team, but I'll have to expand my group of friends, and in a town this size, it's difficult." How could she ask people she hardly knew to help her for free; paying them would be out of the question. Unless she could offer them something worthwhile in return, but what?

"Don't worry about it now. You run upstairs and get ready. I'll work on getting things together down here, then we'll head over to the picnic and set up. I think once the crowd gets a taste of your food, you'll have volunteers jumping at the chance to help." She spun Misty around and began shoving her toward the steps. "Put on a cute outfit and let's get a move on."

Misty skipped up the steps with renewed enthusiasm. What a strange morning it had been. Starting with the phone call from— Carly! How could she have forgotten her best friend was on a bus heading to Crystal Cove for a visit.

Carly. Could this be an I-miss-you, I-haven't-seen-you-in-so-long visit, or was it something more? Her gut said there was more to the story than Carly let on—and it probably involved a guy. As she undressed in the bathroom, she caught a glimpse of herself in the mirror. She wasn't really showing yet, but she would be soon. She ran her hand over her stomach. *Who are you in there?* She couldn't wait to meet him or her in person. There was so much to do in the house to prepare for the baby's arrival. Even after the required repairs, she had painting and decorating to accomplish.

She reached for the faucet and turned on the shower, then waited for the water to heat up before stepping into the white claw-foot tub and closing the plastic, pink curtain. Looking at the faded wallpaper and everything else in the room, she realized how it needed to be updated like almost everything in the entire house. Her heart began to pick up speed and a feeling of being overwhelmed washed over her. *One project at time and it'll be finished before the baby arrives. Maybe.*

She showered in record time, dressed, and was back in the kitchen before Arlene had pulled half of the supplies out of the pantry.

"Here, let me do that. I know where everything is." It was easier to gather what she needed and let Arlene make the trips to the truck. They could save time that way.

After multiple trips to the truck, Arlene sounded slightly

winded when she said, "You sure we got everything?" The heat had already begun to intensify, no doubt foreshadowing what they could expect later on that day. It was going to be a hot one even though the sky had turned overcast.

"I think so." Misty gathered the last of the supplies, going over the list in her head one more time as she locked the door behind her. Excitement and jitters mashed together. In a few hours, she'd find out what the rest of the town thought of her new and improved barbecue pulled pork, beef brisket, and chicken recipes.

"I have a feeling we're going to get more than enough volunteers for your support team." Grinning, Arlene reached for the final shopping bag, resting by the door, and followed Misty over to the truck before sliding inside.

Misty climbed into the driver's seat, closed the door, and let the cold air relieve her damp, overheated skin. "I'd kiss the man that invented air conditioning if he were alive right now."

Arlene's support at a time when the McCabe's had all but dismissed Misty, touched her heart, but at the same time, she simmered inside with the need to be independent— free from the years of struggling to make ends meet. She didn't want her baby to grow up with the kind of childhood she'd had—relying on hand-me-downs, wondering if she would have school supplies, and hoping the other children didn't notice her lack of, well, everything. Tears sprinkled her lashes. It wasn't exactly true. She did have her grandmother's love growing up. Her hormones were getting out of control again. She wanted this day to end before it even really began.

Debra Fisk

The sweet smell of hickory smoke and brown sugar filled the air. Bronson kept his distance from Misty in the silent hope that his feelings for her would subside. He watched her from the farthest corner of the picnic area while she worked her magic. His stomach wanted to swallow up the scent that drifted his way.

The local ranchers, Reese, Braxton, and his workers surrounded her, eager to give her a hand in any way they could. She didn't need his help, and he certainly didn't need to have his heart a few steps closer to love. By avoiding her altogether, he was convinced his feelings would fade in time as they had for Delilah. Misty would eventually find someone else. Yes, Bronson decided his feelings would fade for her much like he'd gotten over

Delilah.

The day had flown by, and he couldn't believe dusk was starting to set in. In another half an hour, he'd get Rad to oversee a few of the other fellas to set up the fireworks. All in all, the day had been a success. All of the puppies had found prospective homes, and from the smile on most everyone's face, they had enjoyed the day. It dawned on him that this was the first picnic Jim had missed since he'd taken over as cook.

Guilt and remorse took over. How could he have forgotten Jim so easily on a day like today?

Misty. He was so busy studying her movements and staying away that he was being downright antisocial. Out of the corner of his eye, he saw a motion, and by the shuffling gait, he could tell Radford was walking up behind him. He was probably looking to him for direction on the fireworks. His brother smacked him on the back.

"Why are you over here by your lonesome?"

"No reason. I was thinking about Jim." Not a total lie—a half truth. "This is the first picnic he's missed since..." His voice trailed off. "Well, you know."

"It is. But that's not why you're over here and you know it."

Busted. He and his brothers could read each other perfectly. There was no hiding a thing from any of them.

"I'm not looking for a relationship, and it was unfair to Misty to…lead her to believe there was something more."

"Really? You just decided that, and you believe you can turn off your feelings like a dripping faucet?" Radford chuckled, and it tripped the pissed-off button on Bronson's temper.

"Look," he snapped, turning to glare at his brother. "I don't need you or Reese or Braxton policing my feelings." He pressed his pointer finger into Rad's chest. "I don't have time for romantic silliness. Jim's been fool enough for all of us."

"You don't say." Rad pushed back, and Bronson realized how ridiculously he was behaving.

"This is what women do: make men crazy and cause a fight."

"Don't go blaming it on anyone but yourself, bro. You're doing it all by yourself. Why, I bet if I hadn't come over here, you'd be arguing with that butterfly over there."

Bronson was acting immature. He wanted to hang his head in shame. Instead, he said, "Go grab the guys and start setting up the fireworks. I'm going to walk off some steam." He grumbled to himself as he walked away.

Taking time and space would do him a world of good. When he returned, he'd grab a plate and eat then watch the fireworks and relax. Things were moving too quickly for a man set in his ways. If the old Jim were here, they'd chuckle about how the other guys were doting on their wives and girlfriends. They'd share how lucky they were to be single—able to do what they wanted—uncomplicated. Now, Jim had gone off and gotten married. His brothers chased every skirt they could, and Bronson was left feeling confused and out of touch for the first time in his life.

His time spent with Misty was easy, enjoyable, and fun. He never once thought of himself as doting or henpecked as some of the guys said. They had a mutual respect and an easy rapport. He laughed with her and could love someone like her. The past four weeks had flown by, to the point where a part of him longed for this to be his new routine—future.

He turned around and looked out, far off in the distance, at the group surrounding her. From his vantage point, dusk made it difficult to see what was going on, but the music could be heard from where he stood and the smell of food floated all the way out that far. She would be better off with someone who could give her the type of family life she needed. He had too many responsibilities and restrictions hampering his ability to lead a normal family life.

Up until now, he'd never given it a lot of thought as to when or if one of his brothers would decide to marry. What would he do? Where would they live? The ranch was their home too. He couldn't ask his brothers to move out of the main house, but how would any of them raise a family there, or what if all three of his brothers decided to bring wives home. There wasn't any privacy in the "big house," as they called it, and he would have to deal with three women trying to take over a kitchen.

Jim had been the first one to break off and marry. Now, he wanted to bring a woman to live at the 4M Ranch. Maybe. He'd never said exactly what he had in mind. All Jim had said was he was ready to come back to work.

Stubbornness had gotten the best of him; now hunger pains changed his mind. It was time to make a plate and chat with Misty.

"I think I'll put my feet in a bucket of ice tonight, Arlene." Misty's throbbing feet pulsated and made her want to sit down and kick off her shoes to escape the burning sensation and freeze them immediately. Arlene had offered to take turns and relieve her for a short break, but Misty opted to keep working. It wasn't that she didn't trust Arlene to watch over the food area; it was more of a comfort-zone issue.

When she did walk away from the cooking line for a few brief moments, she found herself wandering around, feeling out of place. Bronson had sent out the dismissed signal loud and clear and she'd received it by his absenteeism from today's event. Her heart shriveled up, deflated. In a way, it was for the best. Her life was about to change drastically in a few months, and Bronson wasn't the type of man to set his pride aside to raise another man's child.

"Don't look now, but Bronson's walking this way. That man is stubborn as the day is long, and I bet starvin' too."

Misty followed Arlene's gaze to see tall, muscular, and handsome Bronson taking long strides to where they stood. Misty studied his broad shoulders and strong arms. *If only they were wrapped around me.* She could use a hug and the support after a long day of hard work mixed with fun.

"What do you mean by stubborn?"

"He's trying to prove to me…you…everyone around him that he's not falling for ya." Arlene pulled the cigarette from behind her ear and aimed it at Misty, tapping her on the blouse to make a point. "He can lie to himself all he wants, but he can't fool me, and you can't keep lying to yourself either."

"Me?" What the heck was Arlene talking about? "I'm not lying to anyone, including myself."

Liar. But Arlene doesn't know that for sure. She's fishing for information.

"I'm not lying to anyone about anything," Misty repeated tersely. *Ugh —well, sorta.* "We had a business relationship. That's all, and I'm fine. Jim's returning, and I can get the repairs done at the house. My life can get back to normal. It was a lot of responsibility taking care of those four men. I'm ready to move forward with my life."

"If you say so. I'll mind my own business—you won't hear another peep about it from me." Her smirking grin grated on Misty's nerves. Arlene thought she knew everything about everyone in Crystal Cove. As the town's main source of gossip, she knew way more about the townspeople than she did her own restaurant menu.

Misty straightened her meat-juice-splattered top, self-conscious about her sloppy appearance. Bronson was closing in; her heart kicked up a few beats. Why let him think she was pining away for him? Act natural and happy. Ignore him. That was her plan. She'd be fine as long as he kept his distance.

His light eyes darkened beneath his scowl as he concentrated on his target: her. She slid her mouth into a grin. *Act natural.*

"Can I interest you in something to eat?" She hoped he was in a better mood than the deep crevice of a frown conveyed. She swept a hand over the stainless steel chafing dishes.

Arlene stepped up behind Misty, peering over her shoulder. "Or some rattlesnake?" She speared a piece of meat on a fork and waved it in front of his face. She chuckled at the surprised look on Bronson's face. "Oh, that's right, you're through with that."

"What the hell is that supposed to mean?" Bronson ground out. His eyes shot back and forth from Misty to Arlene.

"Gimme that." Misty swiped the fork out of Arlene's hand. "Rattlesnake's not a choice!" Safely tucking a stray piece of hair back behind her ear, she turned to Bronson. "Ignore her. I think the heat's getting to her." She speared daggers at Arlene with a scowl. Why was the older woman baiting him? What could she gain by getting him agitated? "Help yourself," she replied. Misty turned to retrieve her cup of ice water. The heat of the long day had left her parched. She drained the cup and refilled it with fresh ice and water from the cooler. Taking a sip, she let a sliver of ice rest against the roof of her mouth in an attempt to cool herself down.

"No problem." Bronson walked around Arlene, who remained silent, and followed Misty's lead. He downed a fast glass of water followed by a full glass of iced tea. He grabbed a plate from the stack on the table and piled it high, adding extra barbecue sauce on the shredded pork.

Then he took a smaller bowl for a side of coleslaw. He made two trips over to a table to set his food down, and Misty was relieved when he was gone.

She scolded Arlene. "What was that all about? Rattlesnake—really?" Was the old woman sipping moonshine out of sight around back?

With a lopsided smile, Arlene shrugged. "It's private. Like a joke."

"Enlighten me," Misty snapped, unamused, tired of Arlene's mind games and plain sick of her snide comments and innuendoes. Arlene might be the only friend she had in the world besides Carly, but a friend should help the situation not hinder it. Maybe it was a combination of things: the pregnancy hormones mixed with the heat and the fact that she was tired, stressed, and emotionally drained. Lately everything seemed to ride on her nerves.

"Someone's a bit of a grouch." Arlene wiped her forehead with a paper napkin she picked up from the table, then tucked it in her bra for safe keeping. "Rattlesnake refers to Delilah. You get the idea. That woman poisoned him and everyone she came in contact with." Arlene tapped Misty on the arm and turned her around. "Look over by the horseshoe toss. Darla's here with her sister. I'll be right back. I've gotta have a word with her."

Misty watched Arlene steer her way through the thick

crowd gathered in the main tent, at far corner of the picnic area, until she had reached Darla. Misty shook her head, watching as Arlene lifted her arms and part of her shirt to allow the misting fans Bronson had rented to cool her off. Arlene stayed planted in front of the fan while she talked to Darla who looked cool and crisp like the heat didn't have any effect on her at all—not a hair out of place; fresh, clean gingham cotton blue and white blouse; and white, sheer cutoff shorts.

Misty mumbled to herself, "If only I could look half as good." She began cleaning up, ready to end this long day with an ice-cold shower, then crash in her air-conditioned room ready to collapse into bed. A gentle nudge and the brush of fur tickled her ankles. She looked down to see several sets of pleading eyes begging for a taste of the freshly cooked meat.

"I think you look fantastic after a day like today." Bronson leaned in close and took the stack of empty trays from her hands. "I'm sorry if I've been out of sorts today. I've got a lot on my mind with Jim's return. I let today's heat and my empty stomach get the best of me. Will you accept my apology?" Of course she would. She was a sucker for a handsome face, especially his. Besides, she needed his support for the state fair and to start her barbecue business. They should remain friends even if her heart wanted something more.

She reached down and handed Lady and two of her pups

some shreds of the plain beef and pork, the fluffy fur balls hungry for their first taste of table food. She turned her attention back to Bronson.

There were too many reasons to stay away from him. If they became something more, she was convinced it would be the end of their friendship for good.

"Of course I will." Not that it mattered. It wouldn't change anything between them. If they remained friends, it was for the best. Once he learned of her pregnancy, he would change his mind about her. She refused to feel pain and hurt brought on by false hope and shattered dreams.

"I know I'm being sensitive and I'm sorry if I came off angry about Jim," Bronson explained. None of it mattered now. Her life would be filled with her new family in a few months, and Bronson would know she had been lying to him from the beginning. She'd been pregnant by another man, and she'd never mentioned a word of it to him. Not that it was any of his business, but out of friendship or the deep connection they shared, all the time they'd spent together, he deserved an explanation. She wanted tell him but didn't know how without hurting him. He was bound to feel betrayed by her secrecy. He'd shared things with her that he'd shared with no other.

"We've both been dealing with a lot this past month. Now I have to face Jim with a wife and find out if he intends to get back to work or maybe leave us altogether. I'm not so sure about this woman. Anyone who'd condone Jim's secrecy with their elopement must have expected some sort of opposition." He raked his fingers through his hair. "I'm worried about Jim. He's like family. I hope her feelings toward him are genuine."

Misty agreed with his concern. A sickening feeling gripped her stomach as his words resurfaced old wounds inflicted by her mother's lying, cheating ways. How many men had Marla used, and later in life, they'd turned the tables back on her. Somewhere, the line between human decency and morality had been crossed then dismissed completely. Could Jim have gotten himself mixed up with a woman like Marla Summers?

"Jim's lucky to have the four of you to look out for him. I'm sure you and your brothers will expose her if she's not."

With that, Bronson grinned. "Heck yeah. You know it." He picked up the two filled boxes and stacked them on top of each other. "Are you staying for the fireworks?" Hope danced in the gunmetal pupils, pleading with her to stay. Exhausted from the cooking and the heat, and the emotional roller coaster of her hormones, she wanted to go home. Fireworks were the last thing she wanted to sit through on a hot evening like this when she could be home showered and in the cool air conditioning. She looked at her watch; she needed to call Carly before it became too late. Misty couldn't wait to see her. The weeks had flown by but it didn't make a difference to

Misty, Carly was her closest friend despite the fact their friendship had been put on hold lately.

She panned the crowd for Arlene, only to discover her and Darla walking quickly in Misty's direction. Darla smiled, chatting with Arlene about something.

They were within earshot when Darla called out, "Hey, you two. I'm here to help." They could have used Darla's help hours ago, but Misty being a do-it-herself kind of girl was used to taking on projects without anyone's assistance.

Misty appreciated the gesture. "Thanks, but there isn't much left to do. I've got this."

Darla glowed with sweetness and fresh country charm. Her shimmering hair glistened as though someone had thrown a pinch of golden glitter on her head and combed it through. Misty wondered if it was Darla's shampoo or Mother Nature's gift of natural brilliance. Her spotless clothes didn't need to end up sprinkled with meat juice and barbecue sauce.

Darla put on a pout with a wounded look in her eyes when Misty rejected her offer.

"Don't be silly, and while I clean up here, you can fill me in about the plans for your support team."

Arlene didn't waste any time, and Misty appreciated her friendship even more. With Arlene's help and a few more hands, she had a real good chance to win the prize money.

Bronson stopped and leaned over Misty's shoulder. "What support team? What's it for?" The masculine scent of musk and spice mixed with hot male desire caused her pulse to rev, intensifying the heat in her already flushed cheeks. How could she control the unsettling effect he had on her? Burying below the surface every speck of attraction pulling her toward Bronson, she bit her lower lip in silent frustration. Better to keep it under wraps than to continue her childish fantasy.

"The fair," she blurted out.

Help from the McCabe brothers would be an added bonus to the plan Arlene had devised. The competition would be fierce, but Misty was too proud to ask Bronson or his brothers for a speck of help. She couldn't. Letting go stung, and she couldn't wrap her head around what hurt more, losing her job or losing the family of brothers she'd grown to love.

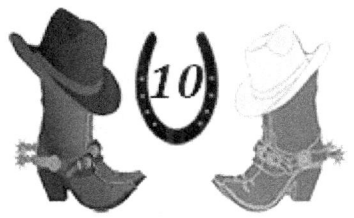

For the first time in her life, Misty was in love, a type of love she'd never imagined possible. The type of love you'd sacrifice everything you owned to protect. Happiness bubbled up inside her. She had waited to feel this type of love her entire life. There was no way to describe it; it was something a person had to experience for themselves. She couldn't tear her eyes away from the glowing image on the screen—strong beating heart, fingers, toes. The cool probe glided across her stomach, taking measurements of the tiny life growing inside her. Her baby. There was her little boy or girl. The technician spoke, but Misty barely heard a word she said as her mind raced with more questions.

"Miss Summers, by these calculations, your baby is right on target at twelve weeks." Using the probe, Bonnie, the technician, stopped then tapped the button to snap a few pictures. Each time she glided the wand left and right, the baby moved away from it. "You've got an active one." Bonnie turned and smiled, wearing an expression of a woman who clearly loved her job.

"I haven't felt a thing." Had she missed feeling her baby move?

Bonnie paused, the machine image frozen on the screen, to take a few more measurements. "Not yet, but soon you will."

The vivid flashbacks of nausea were all too fresh in her head. "At least I'm over the morning sickness." She shivered at the thought.

Bonnie stopped what she as doing for a brief minute. "If I can tell the sex of the baby, do you want to know?"

Did she want to know? She had no one to share it with, at least not until Carly arrived later today. Oh, how she wished her grandmother were alive. "Possibly. I'm not sure. Let me think about it. I can wait a while." Deep down she secretly hoped she could share the baby's sex with Bronson. She let her mind slip into a fantasy: Bronson with her in the doctor's office, learning the sex of her baby; Bronson's loving gaze caressing her face, the two of them about to be parents. If only that could be her future. Their future—together.

"Doctor Kendall has a series of questions for you to

answer," Bonnie said, wiping the gel off Misty's stomach. "I've snapped a few pictures for you to take home." Handing them to her, Bonnie finished helping Misty off the table. She followed Bonnie to another room where she so she could sit and wait for the doctor. Bonnie stayed for a minute, making a few notations in Misty's chart. "He'll be with you in a few minutes." She closed the chart with a smile, stood, then she left, closing the door behind her.

Misty lifted the photos and ran her fingers over them, relieved her baby looked perfect and healthy. Waiting in the doctor's office, Misty had never felt so alone. While other women had their mothers to share their experiences with and ask questions, she had no one.

She hadn't thought about her mother in years, and to tell the truth, she didn't care where she was. The small insignificant relationship they'd once had had fizzled out the night her mother had driven off with a man who could keep the party going. Misty never knew who her father was, but it didn't matter now. For all she knew, he could have died years ago. The entire side of her father's medical history was blank in her file, and her mother's information was equally as sparse. Sadness squelched the joy she felt—now her baby would have a blank father history as well.

Should she break the cycle and tell Beau? Kicking the thought aside, she looked about the room. Where was the doctor?

Staring at the baby growth charts on the wall, she
followed the conception to twelve weeks development
and ran her fingers over the actual-size image. The chart
said her baby was about the size of a plum. Looking at
the growth images on the diagram, the word miracle
stood out in her head.

The door opened, and the doctor stepped into the room.
"Misty, good to see you."

"Hi, Doctor Kendall." Misty made her way over to a
chair and sat back down.

"How are you feeling?" He walked over to the sink to
wash and dry his hands. Then he looked over the notes
and pictures Bonnie had placed on the counter. He was a
man in his early sixties, but he looked like a young
version of Kris Kringle—short beard, slim with a thicker
midsection, salt and pepper hair with black-framed
glasses from the 1950s.

"I'm feeling fine, a little tired at times and the heat
doesn't help."

"Dehydration is a big concern here in Florida, and a
pregnancy multiplies the risks. You'll need to drink
plenty of water during these hot months." He added a few
notations to her patient history.

"I left the baby's father information blank," she blurted

out. Damn, why the heck had that slipped out?

Doctor Kendall raised his eyebrows. "Do you want to talk about it?"

She really didn't want to explain anything to him or anyone else. "I-I know who the father is, but I haven't told him I'm pregnant." She didn't want Doctor Kendall to think she belonged on an episode of the Maury show.

He peered over his black-rimmed glasses. "I understand, and that's your decision." There was a long pause, and the silence made her cringe inside. He took off his glasses and placed them on the counter. "This is your life and your child's. All of the decisions made from this point forward are up to you." That last remark surprised her and gave her the comfort she needed.

Part of Misty wanted to explain, but she chose to hold her tongue. Doctor Kendall continued to give her a verbal list of dos and don'ts for the next stage of her pregnancy.

By the time her appointment ended, a mild grade of guilt and panic had set in. Maybe she should tell Beau? He did have a right to know about his child. Would her baby grow up wondering who their father was and would her child seek him out? Doctor Kendall hadn't condemned her for not telling Beau like she'd imagined he would. Others might not be as forgiving. It was a lot to think about.

On the drive home, she remembered how she'd felt

Debra Fisk

growing up without a father, and those feelings of being an outcast in the community. Misty still had time to decide. Maybe Carly could shed some light on what she should do.

She made it back to town just in time to see the bus pull up at the bus stop. Carly and the driver stepped off and walked around the side where he opened a compartment and removed her suitcases before placing them on the curb. Misty hurried to park Arlene's car and leaped out of the vehicle, heading toward her friend.

"Carly!" she yelled, rushing over to hug the friend she missed so much.

Carly turned and squealed, "Misty!" She reached out to hug her in return. "It's so good to see you. You look fantastic." Carly gave her the once-over, with a huge grin on her face. She grabbed Misty's arms and held them out so she could further look her up and down. The denim sundress Misty wore was form-fitted, and she knew she barely showed any signs of pregnancy at all.

"So how are you, really?" Always a skeptic, Carly didn't waste any time beginning her interrogation.

"I'm fine. We're both fine," she said, glancing down at her stomach. "Now that you're here, things are perfect."

Carly looked worn out, as if she hadn't gotten much sleep on the long bus ride, unless there was some other trouble causing her to look tired and stressed. Misty hoped it wasn't too serious.

After helping Carly with her bags, Misty looped her arm around Carly's and turned toward the truck. "Come on. I bet you're hungry. We can get you settled into one of my guest bedrooms. I can't wait to show you the house."

"Sounds perfect." Carly put her bags into the back of the vehicle, and they both got inside. Misty switched on the air conditioning, then drove the short distance to the house on Galloping Hill and pulled into the driveway.

"It still needs a lot of work," Misty explained, stepping out of the car and placing her hands on the roof. She looked at her sad house that needed a lot of TLC.

"Nice oak trees, and my, what a cute porch swing," Carly said, taking her suitcases out of the back and placing them on the ground. "We can get it fixed up."

"We? Wait. What's going on, Carly?" That telling statement confirmed for Misty that this was more than a social visit. "Is everything okay?" Walking around to the passenger side, she stood next to Carly. Other than the dark circles under her eyes, Carly hadn't changed.

"I'm here to get this place in shape." She dragged her bags, pushed open the dilapidated gate, and walked up the steps, shuffling onto the porch. Misty quickly followed behind her, placing the key in the lock. In the heat, the wooden door had a tendency to swell, and she had to use her hip to shove it open.

"When I arrived, it was exactly as I remembered it as a child."

Misty held the door for Carly while she shoved the bags inside. The lingering odor of barbecue hit Misty hard, and she wondered if she'd ever be able to get rid of that smell. If the weather ever cooled down, she could air out the house.

"Smells delicious in here. Great AC too." Carly moved about the room, looking around. "With a little redecorating, this place will be the perfect home to raise your baby." Her large blue eyes sparkled as she nodded her approval. She turned to Misty and reached out to give her another hug. "I was so worried about you. I didn't realize how much I would miss you until you were gone. The diner wasn't the same without you there giving me your disapproving look every morning when I showed up late."

"I could give you a disapproving look right now…for keeping secrets," she said, trying to gauge Carly's reaction. The flicker in her friend's eyes told Misty she had struck a nerve. She made a motion with her hand. "I'm so lucky to have this home, even with all the repairs it needs."

It was once so beautiful, with a lush green lawn surrounded by a wrought iron gate, overflowing flower beds, and the white paint had gleamed in the sunlight. The large oak trees shaded a good portion of the house and added to the warm feeling. Determined to restore every bit of her grandmother's house, she imagined it completed. Now, if she could win that prize money to do it.

After getting settled in, freshening up, and taking a rather lengthy nap, Carly's demeanor hadn't changed.

"Still tired?" Misty turned away from the stove, shifting toward where Carly sat at the kitchen table. "And I'm the pregnant one." She still wondered what had prompted Carly's visit all of a sudden. "I thought the long nap would have helped."

Carly sat slumped in the kitchen chair with her head resting on the table, her eyes fixed on Misty, but she could tell Carly's thoughts were somewhere else.

Carly lifted her head with a long yawn and stretched. "I think breakfast makes a perfect dinner. I didn't realize I'd slept so late." Her bright-colored yoga shorts and tank top looked like she was about to go for a run instead of just waking up.

"I'm sorry. I know it's way past lunch but breakfast is all I have at the moment. I used every bit of refrigerator space for Bronson's picnic, and to tell you the truth, I really didn't care to see another piece of meat for a few days." She'd finally been able to get the smell of barbecue out of her hair, if not the scent still lingering in the air.

At the mention of Bronson, Carly perked up and her eyes narrowed. "So tell me about this Bronson," she said, looking for more than there really was, folding her arms across her chest.

"There really isn't much to tell." She didn't want to admit she was in love with Bronson, but all the while her brain screamed, *"Liar."* "I cooked for them until Jim came back. It worked out for me. They needed the help and I needed money."

Sigh. Jim should be back by now. She hadn't heard from Bronson since she'd left the picnic two days ago. He said he'd call, but her phone had never rung or indicated a text. She tried to bury the disappointment threatening to bubble to the surface and failed.

She turned her attention to the omelets, bacon, and hash browns cooking on the stove.

"I'm not usually a breakfast person, as you know, but since I've been pregnant, I crave the most unusual foods." She'd always heard rumors of cravings, but figured most women made a lot of it up to get attention. Now she knew it to be true.

"I can eat breakfast any time of the day. Wow, that maple bacon smells so good." Carly licked her lips.

For the first time, Carly looked alert, like the friend she'd left back in Texas. Dying to get to the heart of the visit, Misty waited until she placed all the food on their plates, then she let Carly relax and begin eating before bringing up the subject again.

Pouring ketchup on her hash browns, she said, "So what gives?" She sat across from Carly, hoping it wasn't too serious, and casually added a dash of hot sauce to her omelet.

Carly ignored the question. "Should you be eating hot sauce while you're pregnant?"

Misty smiled at the way they resumed their friendship as if they'd never been apart. Something was up; of that, Misty had no doubt. And it must be more serious than guy trouble, but she'd start there and figure out the issue eventually.

"I'm fine—and don't avoid my question." Holding Carly with a hard stare, Misty waited patiently for an answer. "Is it a guy?" It usually was, but why was this time different? Taking a bite of her omelet, she let the melted cheese hit her taste buds before continuing. Aiming her fork at Carly like a weapon, she said, "Tell me what's going on…now."

Carly's shoulders slumped. "Kinda—sorta, yes and no." She ate a hearty forkful of hash browns smothered in ketchup.

"That explains a lot."

Taking a sip of coffee, Carly continued, "I was dating this new guy—"

"Wait, what happened to—" For the life of her, Misty couldn't remember his name.

"Loser." Carly sighed.

"The new or the old?"

"Both." Propping her elbow on the table, she rested her head in her hand. "Axel, my new guy, convinced me to break up with my boyfriend—Wade. I gave up my apartment and moved in with him. Then he left me for a skanky redhead in less than three weeks. No offense."

"None taken. Mine's more like strawberry blond anyway." This was turning into the house of broken hearts. "But you weren't in love with him. I mean, it was only two weeks."

"Almost three," Carly corrected. "That left me homeless, and no, I wasn't in love. Extreme like…and I couldn't go back to Wade." Her eyes widened with surprise. "Can you believe he moved on to someone else! Talk about my bruised ego. I'm finished with men." Carly made a distasteful frown.

"Ha—I doubt that!" Not that Carly was like Marla Summers, but grownup Misty had been spoon fed on the same false comments until *I'm through with men* turned into *through with you* and her mother took off. "You'll be fine in a few weeks."

"I don't think so." Carly worked on her breakfast/dinner like she hadn't eaten in a decent meal in weeks. "I didn't know you were such a good cook."

"I didn't either. I'm learning out of necessity and I enjoy it."

"So you don't mind if I crash here for a few until I get it together?"

"Of course not. I can use the company and the help." Especially now that she was unemployed, her hectic schedule had slowed down with periods of emptiness.

Jim should be settled in and back to his usual routine. The happy reunion should have taken place by now, also the adjustment of Jim's wife moving in. She shook off the pang of loneliness; she had good friends like Carly and Arlene…even Darla. Friends that were more like family. They would be the only family she had until her baby arrived. She went over to the kitchen counter where she'd placed the pictures from her ultrasound. "Meet Baby Summers," she said, handing them to Carly. "Seeing the baby for the first time made it so real." It was nice to be able to share the excitement with Carly.

Switching her mood to serious, Carly moved closer to reach out and touch Misty on the arm. "You're not alone. You do know that, right?"

Misty nodded, pressing down the sadness, relieved Carly was there to distract from the absence of Bronson. "Thank you."

The doorbell rang, and they jumped in unison.

"Great." Misty wasn't expecting anyone.

Who could that be? Haggard in stained old clothes and a frayed terrycloth robe, she started for the door, snatching the ultrasound pictures from Carly's hands and shoving them in a kitchen drawer.

"Were you expecting anyone?" Running nimble fingers through her hair, Carly tried to right the bedhead hairdo she'd sported since her nap.

"No."

Whipping off her robe, Misty balled it up while shoving it the hall closet then went to see who'd rung the bell. She half expected Arlene, who had a habit of showing up unexpectedly. Instead, when Misty opened the door, Bronson stood there in a navy T-shirt tugged tightly across his arms and chest. His rock-hard muscles filled up the doorframe. Misty nearly got light-headed from the ripped biceps and abs pressing through his taut shirt. Like a sex-starved teenager, she wanted to run her hands over his tight body.

"What are you doing here?" she demanded. It came out a bit harsher than she'd intended, because he'd flustered her, sending hormones rushing through her. A subtle hint of spice blended with woodsy undertone triggered an erratic heartbeat, while her cheeks grew flushed.

He knitted his eyebrows together, looking down at her from beneath his hat. "Hello to you too." He relaxed his stance. "I thought I'd come by and start the repairs on the roof."

"Why didn't you call first?" Not that it would have mattered; depending on where her cell phone was in the house, it didn't get the best reception, and the house phone wouldn't work until she could afford the deposit.

"I tried. No answer. Can I come in?" He lifted his gaze over her head, staring past her.

Carly's voice purred in the background. "Misty, why don't you let him in? Are you hungry? We're having breakfast for dinner."

Misty jumped as Carly's index finger dug into her side. "Ugh. Sure, come in. All the cool air is going out. Are you hungry? I made extra." She didn't want him to know her pantry was pretty bare.

"No thanks. Jim will have dinner when we get back," he said, stepping inside while Misty shut the door behind him. His words stung her heart. Jim was cooking for the family she loved. *Loved!* Who was she kidding? At some point, she'd fallen in love with him and the family of brothers.

Carly extended her hand. "I'm Carly. Nice to meet you."

Bronson took her hand in his and gave it a brief shake. "Carly." He turned back to Misty. "Radford and Reese are meeting me here. We'd like get your roof fixed."

What the heck had prompted that?

"Oh, I had Levi giving me an estimate." She needed his help. Even if she won the prize money this month, there was so much work to be done around the house that the money would fizzle out before she knew it. She took a deep breath and let it out. "Thanks, that would be a big help."

"We can save you some money. We'll work for food." He grinned. "You can feed us later."

Her heart soared. "But I don't understand. You have Jim back. Why do you need me to feed you?" The unusual request puzzled her.

"I wouldn't come right out and say this in front of Jim"— Bronson's eyes sifted to Carly and back to Misty—"but me and the guys think your cooking is the best food we've tasted since…like ever."

Her cheeks burned at the compliment. "I don't know what to say."

"You can say yes."

"Won't Jim be upset?"

"Jim's in love. I don't expect the two of them to stay at the ranch too much longer. From what I gather, they're going to look for their own place. I get the feeling they'd like to be alone."

"I can understand that," Carly added. "If I was a newlywed, why would I want to live with a house full of guys?" Carly's face of disgust almost made Misty laugh. "Cleaning up after them. Ahh, no thank you." She turned and walked back into the kitchen without waiting for a response.

"Carly's staying with me for a while." For some reason she felt the need to share that with him. Two unemployed women, living in a house that needed a host of repairs probably looked like a hard-luck case to him. "How are the puppies doing?" She wanted to shift his focus from her depressed state to a happier topic. She missed the interaction with little fur balls she'd helped bring into the world. Soon they would be old enough to go to their forever homes.

"Just as cute as can be. Growing bigger and bolder every

day."

The sound of a truck pulling into the driveway caught their attention. "Sounds like your brothers are here."

"Why, yes, it does. We'll get started right away, and I apologize in advance for the noise." He turned and let himself out while Misty scanned his broad back as he headed down the porch steps. She needed a cold drink to cool off her overheated hormones. She returned to the kitchen where Carly was spying out the window at the McCabe men pulling their T-shirts over their head.

"There's something about a shirtless, sexy cowboy in jeans and a tool belt. Excuse me while I wipe the drool off the window. Wanna take a peek?"

"No, thank you." Pouring a glass of lemonade, the tart-sweet mixture didn't satisfy like being doused with a bucket of ice water would. "I thought you were through with men."

Carly rolled her eyes. "I am, but it doesn't hurt to look. I'm not dead." Her words were muffled from where she rested her elbows on the wooden window ledge and pressed her face up against the glass.

In a few seconds, thumping and hammering echoed through every room in the house as the three brothers went to work. If the sound was deafening on the lower level, she couldn't imagine what it sounded like upstairs. Misty walked back over to the table, determined to finish her breakfast/dinner. Afterward, she would clean up the dishes then…what—read? She could hardly think with a noise level that compared to a war zone! A vision of Bronson on the roof, dressed in tight jeans—shirtless—in a cowboy hat made her want to think of an excuse to go outside.

Daydreaming of sun-bronzed muscles rippling as he swung a hammer up on the roof caused her to grab a napkin and dab the back of her neck and forehead. Wow, she needed to cool down. With her attraction growing from bad to worse, a crushed heart loomed in the future.

Carly spun around to face her. "I bet these guys are thirsty. Iced tea or lemonade?" She moved to the refrigerator and stood with the door wide open.

"Either one is fine. Whatever we have more of." In this heat, Carly should serve them each a pitcher of their own. Florida heat was about the same as Texas heat, but you had to account for the added humidity. In Texas, the dry heat was like baking in an oven, while the hot humid temperatures in Florida sucked the body's energy. None of the brothers would turn down either offered drink.

Selecting a jug of iced tea and placing it on the counter, Carly asked, "Got a tray?" She removed three glasses from out of the cabinet.

"Bottom right." Misty pointed to the lower door on the end. Carly filled the glasses, dropped in a lemon wedge, and loaded the tray, smiling the entire time. Misty held the back door open and Carly headed outside. There was no way Misty was going out there. The temptation to touch his hard, tan muscles was too great, and those were feelings she did not want to encourage. Distance was the only way to save herself.

She heard the front door open and heavy footsteps run up the stairs.

"Carly!" she yelled instinctively, knowing there was no way it could be her. She couldn't have made it around the house that fast. "What's wrong?" She raced up the stairs, following the footsteps toward the attic.

"Misty, don't come up here," Bronson commanded, freezing her in place by the severity of his tone. Something was drastically wrong. "I'll be down in a minute to explain."

Standing at the edge of the attic stairs, she could feel the extreme heat rolling down the steps and wondered how Bronson could stay up there more than a few seconds. She ran to the bathroom and grabbed a towel. He'd probably need to dry himself off from the amount of perspiration dripping down his chest in that heat.

"Are you all right?" she called up the stairway, worried he'd passed out.

Heavy boots started down the steps; she handed him a towel when he reached the bottom. "Thank you," he said, taking the towel from her hands. He dried his head, chest, and back. "You've got a slight problem up there. I hate to tell you this." He paused, heightening her level of alarm. "You have a small colony of bats. Nothing to worry about; it's not a big one. We can handle it." Tossing the towel over his shoulder, he placed one hand on the wall for support and the other on his hip. Close—bare-chested and incredibly sexy—she fought to keep her eyes on his rather than scan his body.

"Bats in the attic? How?"

He slammed the attic door and locked it. "We're gonna get rid of them. We wouldn't want them to start to make their way downstairs."

"How are they living up there in this heat?" Pressing her stomach to suppress the urge to gag at the discovery. "Gross." She wasn't afraid of animals in their natural habitat—but in her house? That was a different story.

"Since bats eat bugs, they must have been busy with this place closed up."

Misty gasped. "What should I do?" She didn't have money for any extreme extermination process. "A bug hasn't crossed my path since I moved in here, which is strange considering how long this place had been empty." Did her grandmother have these pests living in her attic and not know it? "How long do you think they've been there?"

"Not long from the small amount of guano. You're lucky we found it now. No matter." He shook his head. "With Radford and Reese, the three of us will make sure they're gone. Even if we have to stay here all night."

Misty bit her lower lip. "Guano?" What the heck was that?

"Their waste...you know, feces. The term is guano, and can grow a fungus that causes lung disease. We're going to need to protect ourselves and you ladies down here."

Misty couldn't believe this. She couldn't expect them to do this dirty work. She felt lower than the bat guano. If they did stay, what about sleep? How would she survive the night with Bronson in the house?

"No! That won't be necessary," she said, grabbing a muscular arm and guiding him toward the steps that lead to the main level. "You've done so much already." She fought the desire to run her hand across his chest. "I think it can wait until tomorrow. Right? I mean...they've been living there for weeks—months maybe—one more night won't make a difference."

Would it? She hoped not, but the thought of him lingering in the attic while she slept below kicked up her pulse. She could ask Levi if he knew how to remove them. She was embarrassed enough by her situation.

The wicked smile he flashed stopped her heart. "I hate to break it to you, darlin', but we've got to remove them at night for several reasons. Once they leave, we'll seal up the holes. In this heat, a third floor attic becomes an incinerator during the day. We wouldn't last more than five minutes up there." The way he said darlin' made her breath catch. He leaned in close. So close she could feel the breeze of his words brush upon her cheek. "Don't worry. We'll be quiet so you ladies can sleep."

Sleep? Ha! Like that could happen. Not when she had been squelching her crush—passion—love for him and had bats hanging in her attic.

"Don't you think you should talk to your brothers first? They must have better things to do—like sleep—tonight. I can get someone in the morning to come over and remove these pests." He was too close. Instinctively, her hands went to his chest, pressing him back. A jolt of sexual current went straight to her groin. Oh boy, this was turning her on.

He locked his gaze with hers. "They'll be fine, besides the two of them are enjoying your friend Carly's hospitality."

"Carly said she gave up men." Apparently ranchers weren't in the excluded group. She leaned back in an attempt to recapture her composure. "Then I guess it's settled. You guys are pulling an all-nighter here." So much for keeping her distance. They should be separated by miles not several hundred feet. She couldn't figure him out. One minute he gave the impression he was into her—flirtatious—and then like the flick of a switch, he turned icy, distant. "I appreciate the help," she whispered.

Bronson gave her an eyebrow wriggle. "It's gonna be a fun night." He then jogged down the steps, taking them two at a time.

She stared at the closed attic door for several seconds after he left. Then she walked slowly down to the kitchen. It was going to be a 'fun night' as he put it, after all.

Bronson and his brothers peeled off the weathered shingles a section at a time. He took a few steps toward a bare patch of exposed wood, but stopped when the roof sagged under his weight. One more step and he could go crashing through the rotten boards and into the attic. He whipped out his cell phone and called Braxton to bring over more supplies.

"The rotted plywood underneath will have to be torn out," he announced to Radford and Reese. "We could patch it, but like Daddy always said, it's better to do something right once than half-ass and have to repeat it."

While they were at it, it was mandatory to replace the dry, sparse insulation in the attic. It would have to be ripped out anyway to be sure they had removed all of the guano. This wasn't the first time they'd run across a situation like this. The barn back at the ranch had bats they needed to remove on occasion.

"I think it's engrained in every one of us," Radford agreed, stripping another section of shingles and throwing them to the ground. He stopped, then looked Bronson in the eye and asked, "Are you going to take Misty out on a date or what?" Leave it to Rad to get right to the point. "I mean, we'd help with the roof and all anyway, but I can tell you have the hots for her, and she does for you too, so stop acting all weird and ask her out already." It sounded more like a plea than a question. "Your sour mood disappears when she's around, so face it, man, and make your move."

Bronson frowned and gave Radford a sarcastic reply. "I hadn't noticed you'd been suffering from my *sour mood.*" Even though Bronson wouldn't admit it to anyone, his mood was sour—for a lot of reasons. Mostly his stubborn pride and skepticism. Clearly, Misty wasn't anything like her mother; she wasn't a liar or deceitful. In fact, from what he could tell, she had a sense of honor and pride that he admired. She'd never once tried to manipulate things to her advantage, and she was a hard worker, taking on more than one job to pay her bills. Not like her mother who looked for a man to foot her bills.

Adding his two cents, Reese commented. "Rad's right.

You are bitter as the day is long." No pressure. His brothers were double-teaming him. Once Braxton arrived, he'd no doubt join in. Bronson would never hear the end of it until he took her out somewhere.

Bronson used a gloved hand to push his hat up. "As soon as we're done here, I plan on fixing that." It wasn't a lie. He'd been going over the pros and cons in the back of his mind since Misty had first arrived in Crystal Cove, fighting his deep attraction for her. No more. They would take things slow and see where it led. He wasn't about to get his hopes up, but it would be nice to have a relationship with a woman for a change instead of hanging around with the guys in his free time.

An hour later, Braxton arrived with the remainder of the supplies, and the three of them climbed down to help him unload the truck. They set up spotlights in preparation for sundown.

With all four men working, they were able to finish the roof before midnight. They had to wait for the bats to fly out before sealing up their passage to the inside. Then they moved into the attic to seal up the hole. Trying to be quiet was next to impossible, but four men in work boots, lugging everything they'd needed, made more noise than even he'd anticipated. When this mess was over, he'd apologize for the noise by taking her out to dinner.

She was alone in her room. He could go knock and apologize in person before he left. Maybe even steal a kiss.

Tossing and turning in bed, Misty forced down the urge to go into the attic and see what the heck was going on. There was a lot of commotion for three guys who claimed she would be able to sleep right through the night, not that she could have even if they were quiet as mice. Their voices traveled through the vents, and she couldn't catch a wink of sleep with the footsteps overhead and the roar of some kind of industrial vacuum. There couldn't be that many bats?

A light tap on the door caused her to bolt upright. "Who is it?" she asked. Bronson? A thrill of excitement shot through her.

"It's me. Carly. Can I come in?" The door opened before Misty could even answer. "I can't sleep. I mean, how many bats can there be?" She walked over to the bed and sat on the edge.

"I was wondering the same thing." Trying not to give off

the impression she was crushing on Bronson, Misty asked, "Now that you've met them, what do you think of the three McCabe brothers?" She got the impression Carly was interested in one of them more than the others. "For someone who gave up on men, you were being quite the little hostess," Misty teased.

Carly laughed. "They're all super-hot. I can see why you arrived in Crystal Cove and never called me. I didn't think it could get any hotter out—but damn—standing next to those two hunks of raw sex outside, the temperature just rose another fifty degrees."

Misty frowned. "I know what you mean. If Bronson stands next to me, I'm melting." She exposed her biggest fear aloud. She was in love, even if it was a mistake to fall for him. She couldn't help who she fell in love with. No one could. "Don't get too close or you might get burned." Her internal temperature rose whenever she stood close to Bronson.

After working there for a few weeks and cooking all of their meals, she pretty much knew who was suitable to date Carly and who was not. "You haven't met Braxton yet, until then don't commit if one of them happens to ask you out on a date."

"What's going on with you and Bronson?" Carly pried, and Misty wasn't about to give an inch.

"I have feelings for him, but nothing can happen with my

situation." The melancholy tone of her voice sound pathetic even to her own ears. "I wish things were different, but they're not. I'm happy about the baby, just not the timing, and that it won't have a father." When she had imagined her future, it was married for a few years, maybe buying home, then having a family. It was funny how life had different plans.

Debra Fisk

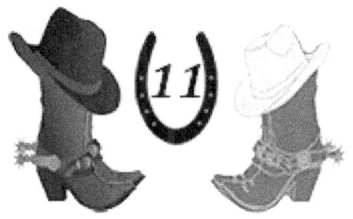

The next morning, with her eyes burning from lack of sleep, Misty dragged her tired body through the doors of the Lakeside Inn right behind Carly. The smell of burgers, fries, and good old grease saturated the air, qualities that made the classic hole-in-the-wall cafe famous in the area.

"Smells yummy." Carly moved off to the side. "After you." She shifted to allow Misty to lead the way over to the counter where Arlene thumbed through the latest issue of Rodeo Circuit Magazine. Misty's weary eyes almost popped out of her head. They were burning before but now they were scorched as the image seared her pupils. Pearly white teeth, strong jaw, blue eyes that made all the women weep stared back at her. The shock of seeing Beau on the cover rendered her speechless. The hunger pains evaporated, twisting her stomach upside down. Her feet came to a screeching halt, and Carly slammed into her back.

"Sorry," Carly mumbled, "I didn't realize your legs forgot how to walk."

Misty mumbled, "Grumpy, aren't we?"

Reluctant to move forward, she stayed firmly planted in place, hypnotized by the cover and Beau's smile. He looked better than she remembered—handsome, rugged, the poster child for the rodeo...and her baby's father.

Carly peered over her shoulder and followed Misty's gaze. A soft, "Oh," floated out of her lips. "At least he's doing well, if, you know..." Carly let her sentence hang unfinished.

"No, I don't know," Misty ground out.

"In case you need help?"

"Like that would even happen." She could never take money from Beau unless she was a willing to share her baby with him, and she wasn't sure she wanted to open that door. Once Beau learned of the baby, there would be no turning back.

Arlene looked up. "Hey, Misty. And you must be Carly." Arlene closed the magazine, but now Beau's face smiled up from the counter. "I heard you had a busy night with bats and the McCabe boys." Arlene could get away with calling them boys, but Misty imagined Bronson without a shirt and envisioned only a full-bodied, hot man.

Carly's jaw dropped. "Wow, news spreads here faster than wildfire."

Misty admitted this newsflash was quick, even for Crystal Cove standards. Arlene rested her arms on the counter, and her hand covered Beau's smile so only his eyes stared up at Misty. She turned her attention back at Arlene.

"How did you find out?"

Arlene pushed her glasses up on the top of her head. "Braxton stopped here to pick up a few sandwiches before driving out to your place last night. Then Jim stopped in with his new bride after that. Jim said he didn't have to cook because the guys were fixing up your place."

True.

They were fixing up her place, and she was grateful, but she didn't want to owe anyone, and right now, she felt like she owed Bronson and his brothers. She had to figure out a way to set things right. There had to be a way to pay them back to even out her obligations.

Arlene picked up the phone, held up an index finger to signal for them to wait, then dialed a number. "Darla, can you come down to the cafe? Misty and Carly are here.

Okay, thanks." Placing the phone on the receiver, she said, "I asked Darla to come here so we can finish our plan for the state fair."

"I know I've been distracted. I need to move quickly. I don't have much time." The weight of her situation hammered her skull, and she wanted to crawl away and hide. Instead, she sucked in a long breath. "You know, it won't be that bad—now that Carly's here."

"I'll volunteer to help."

Misty recognized the weathered voice behind her as Levi Gilligan. She hadn't heard from Levi since she had asked him to bid on the roof.

"I know I can round up a few more folks willing to help." Levi looked tired.

"Are you all right?" Misty asked, realizing he wasn't as she looked into his eyes.

He pushed his hat high above his eyebrows. "I've been better, but I'll live." He gave her a wink. "Just a bit worn out."

"I never heard from you about my roof." If he didn't want the job or was too busy, he should have been upfront about it.

Levi tilted his head and shrugged. "I knew it was getting taken care of so I didn't have to worry."

"What do you mean?"

Arlene made a scathing comment. "I'll tell you what it means. He was passing the buck off."

Levi snapped, "Shut your trap, Arlene. You don't know nothin'." Turning back to Misty, he replied, "That's not true." Levi shifted his eyes, cleared his throat, then leaned in closer as if he were about to disclose a secret. "I promised Bronson I wouldn't mention it, but he stopped by my house the day after I came out to your place and paid me for my trouble. He said he'd take care of the repairs. To tell you the truth, I'm getting a little too old to be on the roof."

Bronson paid Levi and told him to forget the work? She hadn't asked Bronson to step in and take over, not that she didn't appreciate his help, but she could manage on her own. Or at the very least he could have consulted her. Levi too old? She wasn't buying it. He'd looked like he could climb up on the roof and repair anything that day.

"You could have let me know somehow," Misty responded. She couldn't really be upset at Levi; he thought what he was doing would help her out. It was actually kind of sweet.

"It won't happen again, I promise." Levi drew an X over his heart.

Arlene huffed. "*Pffft.* Whatever. Can we get back to the support team?"

Carly snatched a menu off the counter. "Can we get some breakfast? I'm starved."

Misty took Levi by the arm. "I need to sit down and eat too. Let's move over here." She led him over to a table, pulled out a chair, then sat down. Levi and Carly did the same.

"What'll ya have?" Arlene folded her arms across her chest and tapped her foot impatiently.

Carly studied the menu. "Let me see—"

Misty rattled off her order. "I'll make it easy. I'll have a big breakfast combo, dry toast with extra bacon, and a glass of juice." After last night, she needed food, and more sleep, then more food. Lately her stomach was like a bottomless pit. The broken sleep didn't help matters. In the past few days, she could feel the effects of pregnancy in her drained energy.

Carly gave up looking and folded the menu closed. "Umm, I'll have the same with coffee." Reaching for the ketchup, Carly set the bottle down in front of Misty.

"Coffee for me," Levi said. The door to the cafe opened and Darla entered.

Arlene turned and waved Darla over. "Hey, girl, just in time. Can I get you something?"

"I'll have coffee with scrambled egg whites." Darla wore a yellow, floral sundress and flat sandals with white rhinestones that made her feet sparkle when she walked toward them with a smile as bright as her outfit. "Morning, ladies, how's it going?"

"Tired. Hey, Darla, like wow, I love the outfit. This is my friend Carly. She's going to be staying with me for a while. We had a long night." That was an understatement, but life wasn't fair, and she had to move forward with her plan for her baby's future.

Arlene hurried off to the kitchen with their orders, and Darla pulled out a chair to sit down. "Hey, Levi. Nice to see you here. Are you going to help?"

Levi grinned. "I'm in."

Misty looked over at Carly who teetered on the edge of falling asleep. "Carly, open your eyes."

Carly's eyelids slowly peeled open. "Cut me some slack. I didn't get a lot of sleep on that bus, like zero, and last night added to the pile of sleepless nights."

Darla knitted her eyebrows together. "What happened last night?"

"Bronson and his brothers came by to help repair my roof, but they found some bats in the attic and that was a mess to clean up. Let's just say Carly and I didn't get much sleep with all the racket in the attic."

Darla frowned. "Sounds like it—four cowboys in the attic and then fixing the roof had to be loud. Men don't know how to be quiet."

Misty agreed. The four men on the roof without shirts had also affected her sleep, especially thoughts of Bronson. He cared enough to help her, but why? Did he think of her as a charity case? Even if he did have an attraction for her—and that was a big *if*—he'd never act on it.

"Woo-hoo, Misty." Darla snapped her fingers in front of Misty's face. "You zoned out."

"Sorry." Misty placed a hand on the back of her neck and massaged her aching muscles.

Arlene returned tableside with a tray of juice and coffee. "Are we ready to begin now?" Setting all the drinks down, she then pulled up a chair and dropped into it. Getting right to the point, she began with a to-do list of things they should move on in the next twenty-four hours, then a list for each day after that with a detailed itinerary. They had no time to waste with less than a week until the fair. "This will set the wheels in motion for Misty to win the grand prize," Arlene was already jacked up the enthusiasm and blurted out, "No one from Crystal Cove has ever won the state fair. Your grandmother came close a few times, but you already knew that."

"I did...from the notes in her book. It's how I discovered the base recipe for the barbecue sauce I created in the first place." If she could win, she could honor her grandmother's memory, restore her home, and be able to provide everything she would need for the baby. She had to win; losing wasn't an option.

Carly sipped her coffee, then said, "You know, when you win, we can really decorate the house, new paint, drapes —really freshen the place up."

"I'd love to help," Darla offered, "I have a lot of experience with decorating. Can I come by when we're done here and see the place to get some ideas?"

Darla had an amazing sense of fashion and style. If she decorated like she dressed, the entire house would look like it was out of a magazine. Misty smiled. "I'd like that."

"Were getting sidetracked," Arlene commanded. "So, Levi, you'll gather everyone you can to join the support team. Darla, same for you. Carly, you're new, so you won't be expected to have your own team, but you'll be there to help Misty." Arlene took out her ordering pad, pulled the pen out from behind her ear, and then jotted a few notes down. "Also, I think we should have matching shirts that read Summer Heat for everyone on the team."

Darla repeated the name. "Summer Heat? I love it. I can get the shirts."

"I was counting on you to say that," Arlene said.

Misty's cheeks burned. The McCabe's wearing shirts that

read Summer Heat would have all the woman swooning as they walked through the crowd. She sipped her juice to cool her excitement, grateful Arlene was working on a solid plan for success. They would give it their best shot; the rest was up to her and the judges.

Moe himself served the food. As Misty ate, her mind wandered back to Bronson and his brothers. She couldn't even have entered the state fair if he wasn't giving her the meat to sell at the competition. Sales would be critical for her success, but could a support team from this tiny town have the power to sway the crowd? Could she work side by side with Bronson without losing the rest of her fragile heart in the process?

Bronson awoke tired, his muscles aching, and with the weight of the ranch workload pressing down on him before he rolled out of bed. The smell of bacon and biscuits drifted up through the vents from downstairs. He had tried to sleep in, but his natural DNA alarm clock wouldn't allow it. He lay in bed for a while, wrestling with the idea of getting up, then flipped off the covers, got dressed, and headed downstairs.

He doubted his brothers would be up this early, but was

surprised when he entered the kitchen to see Reese sitting at the table eating. Lady and her puppies bunched around the lower portion of his chair. The little furry crowd waited patiently for a small taste of bacon or sausage, while Jim cooked more at the stove.

Bronson raked a hand through his hair. "Morning."

"Morning," Jim and Reese said in unison.

Jim turned away from the stove toward Bronson. "Have a seat. I'll fix you a plate."

Reese fed a smidgen to Lady and each one of the pups.

Reese motioned toward the fuzzy pups. "I know they've been a lot of work, but I'm gonna miss these puffs of fur when they go to their forever homes."

Bronson watched the smallest pup try to push its way closer to Reese but was pressed out by the others. It reminded him of Misty; the little one had a special place in her heart. He went over and picked it up.

"This tiny girl's so darn cute." Looking to share a bit love, the pup gave Bronson an affectionate lick on the cheek. She nuzzled against the side of his face and he caught a whiff of her puppy breath. "This teeny one is special."

"I think they're all special," Jim said, walking over to the table with a plate. "Here ya go, filled with all of your favorites." He set it down in front of Bronson. Placing a kiss on the puppy's nose, he pulled out a chair, placed the wiggly puppy on the floor, then sat down.

"Just what I need to jumpstart my day." Bronson stabbed his fork into the pile of scrambled eggs while Jim made himself a plate and sat down.

"Just like old times, well sorta." Jim wrinkled his face then added, "I'm sorry I left you guys in a lurch. I hope you'll understand. Forgive me?"

Bronson did understand. He didn't like it, but how could he fault the man who'd stepped in and held their family together after each loss of their parents. "Jim, there's nothing to forgive. You've devoted your entire life to this family. It's about time you found some happiness." Bronson spoke from his heart. He really did want Jim's happiness.

The older man smiled. "Now that I have Pauline... We think it's best if we find a place of our own. Living at the ranch isn't the kind of life suitable for newlyweds, if you know what I mean." Jim waggled his eyebrows to emphasize his point. Bronson received the message loud and clear.

Reese stopped eating and set his fork down. "I had a feeling you'd be leaving." Getting up to get another cup of coffee, Reese looked back over his shoulder to make sure none of the dogs were going to steal food off his plate. "I don't blame you for getting tired of hanging out with us guys. I guess when you start getting old, you look to settle down."

Bronson sighed. Everything was going from bad to worse. "I can't fault ya. If I had to decide whether to live with my wife or stay on the ranch with a bunch of men, I'd leave too."

Soft footsteps sounded from the hallway, and Pauline appeared in the doorway, smiling. The three men turned and stared at her, then mumbled, "Morning."

Pauline's smile faded. "Morning." She directed her next comment to Jim. "I take it you told them."

Bronson understood why Jim was attracted to Pauline—shapely body with dark chin-length hair and sable eyes, in her mid-forties, so a bit younger than Jim. They looked like they were made for each other. Bronson's parents could communicate with their eyes, and Jim and Pauline appeared to have that same kind type of connection. Sorta like Bronson had with Misty, but that was different. She knew food, and was a damn good cook, and he knew how to enjoy it. She was interested in him, working to improve her situation not trying to snag a husband for financial support.

In fact, he noticed her independence. Misty didn't ask for things to be given to her. Instead, she worked hard and had arranged for her supplies to be on credit. He'd been a little leery at first, considering her background, but now he knew her well enough. She was nothing like her mother. She was genuine, honest, and truthful. Could she be the perfect woman for him? Deep down in his heart, he felt she might just be. Did Misty have feelings for him?

The car lurched forward, and she heard a soft "*uff*" from Carly in the backseat. Darla didn't make a sound, but she gripped the passenger side door to steady herself against the jolting movement. The front tire had ground into a pothole in her driveway created by one of the trucks driven by the McCabe brothers yesterday. Gripping the steering wheel, Misty said a silent prayer the drop hadn't broken the axel or left the tire flat.

"Sorry, guys," she apologized to her two passengers.

"I'm fine," Carly replied.

"Me too," Darla assured her. The crevice had grown deeper whenever the tire hit the edge. It was a small price to pay for the benefits she'd received. Bronson and his brothers had saved her thousands on a new roof, plus her home was free from bats and leaks. Feeling like a driver's ed student for no reason other than her own insecurities,

Misty had been careful to avoid the gaping crater earlier but had since forgotten it was there. Her mind had been preoccupied with Darla coming over to give her house a redecorating overview.

She struggled to control her frazzled nerves as she threw the car in park. She could use some of Darla's creative decorating talent. It was difficult to bring someone who grew up blessed like Darla to her home. The sympathy on her face when they pulled up to the Summers house on Galloping Hill Road said it all. Darla analyzed the exterior while she hip-bumped the car door closed.

"I remember what this placed used to look like years ago. From the road, you can't tell how much it's deteriorated. It looks worse the closer you get."

Misty's spirits slumped. "Tell me how you really feel." Hearing Darla state the obvious hurt, even though there was no hint of malice in her voice.

Darla lived in one of the most beautiful homes Misty had ever seen. Growing up, Darla and her sister had had slumber parties and elaborate birthday bashes at their family estate. Those few moments were some of the best in Misty's life.

Darla made her way to the front door then stopped and placed her hands on her hips while Misty unlocked the door. "You know the place is charming. I can really envision a mixture of contemporary and classic." She ran her hand along the woodwork while she roamed through the lower level with Misty and Carly trailing silently in her wake.

"Can I see the upstairs?"

Misty nodded. While they continued the tour of the upper level, Darla folded her arms across her chest, ready to give her assessment. "It's structurally sound, with a few areas that need attention and some paint, but this place will be perfect for you."

Misty agreed the house was perfect, but she didn't want to remove of all of her grandmother's possessions. The place had to feel like hers—a real home for her baby—but somehow she needed to blend her grandmother's things with a fresh vision. So much of her life had changed. There were lots of decisions to make. Carly and Darla discussed what should go to Goodwill and what should stay. Some sentimental items would be boxed for the attic.

Misty blurted out, "I don't want to get rid of everything that was my grandmother's." Holding on to the stored possessions gave Misty a sense of closeness to her grandmother.

"Of course not, silly." Darla hooked Misty's arm in hers. "I wouldn't dream of it. Why don't we start with one room, remove what furnishings and soft items that aren't needed while you go through the personal effects."

Carly knitted her eyebrows. "Soft items?"

"That's an interior designer's term for any non-furniture items—drapes, throw pillows, linens, etc.," Darla explained. "Misty you might want to keep them in storage, but for the sake of decorating, I'd like to strip each room down as much as possible. Then I can work my magic."

Darla pulled her cell phone out of her pocket and walked through the rooms, recording her thoughts then stopping periodically to type in a few notes. Misty and Carly tagged behind her, and Misty gained a new perspective of how each room could blossom under Darla's creative touch.

"I know what I have to do." Misty would remove the unnecessary remnants in the rooms. "I need to make piles of the items I don't want, then we can decide what will stay."

The three woman moved through the house like a decorating task force. Misty selected the must-keep items, then Darla gave directions with what remained about which were to be tossed, given to Goodwill, and they sorted it all into piles. Several hours passed, but they only took a break for refreshments then went back to work.

Misty walked over to an old cedar trunk up against the wall in the bedroom that was hers years ago. A few dolls sat on top and Misty remembered how she'd loved those dolls growing up. Her grandmother was always ready to stop what she was doing for a doll tea party. Misty lifted each one of the dolls carefully off the trunk and placed them on the bed. These would definitely go in the "keep" pile. She opened the chest to find it filled with sentimental items. There were worn-out school papers and report cards, both her mother's and hers. Pictures Misty had drawn for her grandmother. There were a few baby dresses, made of fine satin with lace trim, and tiny shoes. Misty wasn't sure which of the clothes were hers or her mother's.

Inside a large box was her grandmother's wedding dress, fully preserved and still looking beautiful. Misty admired the stunning white gown made with gorgeous, delicate lace and a thin line of glittering beads around the neckline. She remembered her grandmother mentioned it was talked about for weeks after the wedding, specifically how excessive her sparkling gown was for that time.

Misty chuckled aloud. "Excessive." That was an overstatement. This gown was simple yet elegant. Misty wanted to wear this dress on her wedding day. At this rate, that would never happen. She gently placed the dress back in the box, glad for a few minutes of silence while her friends were off in another part of the house. This wasn't how she'd imagined her life. She'd wanted to be married someday to raise a family, not the other way around. How she would love to wear that wedding dress with Bronson waiting down the aisle.

"Oh, there you are."

Startled by Carly's voice, Misty snapped her head around to stare at her friend. "What's wrong?" She rubbed her nose in pretense that her sniffles were from the dust rather than the emotion of finding the pristine wedding dress.

"Nothing, I was just checking on you. You're not overdoing it, are you?"

Misty placed the box back in the chest and closed the lid before Carly could see what she'd found. "I'm fine." She had every intention of being cautious around Carly who acted like an overprotective mother. "Thank you. There's no reason to panic. I'm not a porcelain doll. I'm not going to break."

Arching her eyebrow, Carly said, "Let's not get snippy, shall we."

Misty took a deep breath and let it out, curbing her sharpness. "You're right." She ran a hand through her hair. "Did you need something? Where's Darla?"

Carly walked a fine line between a busybody and devout friend. Some secrets weren't meant for best friends; they should remain private. Misty didn't want to share her emotions concerning the wedding dress—at least not yet.

"Right here." Darla appeared in the doorway behind Carly. "So, are you ladies ready to select paint colors?" She waved her iPhone in her hand. "I've pulled up some ideas to help narrow it down. Then we can go on a road trip to pick up swatches and some samples."

Carly looked surprised. "Road trip?"

"There aren't any paint stores here in town," Misty explained. In fact, there wasn't much of anything in town. This was the perfect, simple life she'd longed to raise her child in—a small town where people were like family. But she still worried they wouldn't accept her and her situation. Sure, this was the twenty-first century, and back in San Antonio, things were different. This was Crystal Cove, and it was as if time stood still here. Life moved at a much slower pace than the big city.

Carly blew out a long breath. "I've noticed not much is around. I thought you lived on the edge of town. Now I know this *is* the town."

"It's kinda late in the day to go now, so let me know when you're free." Darla looked at her phone and scrolled her thumb across the screen as she walked into the room. "It looks like I'm free most of next week."

Misty rolled her eyes at Darla. "I'm not. Remember the state fair. Hello." Misty waved her hand in front of Darla's face. "The fair you've agreed to help with."

"I don't know why it's not showing up on my calendar.

Of course I'm helping." She began to tap her screen again. "There, it's all set. I'm in."

Misty heard the low rumble of a truck engine, then the sound of tires grinding into the gravel driveway. The three of them walked toward the front window to see who was outside. Behind the wheel of the truck was Bronson with his brother Reese. They pulled a twelve-foot trailer behind the truck.

Darla shoved the drapery aside to get closer look. "What in the world is he doing now?" She went downstairs, walked toward the front door, and swung it open. "Hey," she called.

"Darla, I can handle this." Misty popped the screen door open with her palm and went outside. "Hey, what are you guys doing?" She bounced down the porch steps and walked over to the truck while the two men started to climb out.

"We're headed to deliver the trailer to the fairgrounds. It's loaded with everything you need, but we're stopping by to see if you needed to add anything." Tipping his hat up, kindness showed in his gray eyes. "What were you ladies up to?" Bronson flashed a grin and her knees wobbled, while Reese walked around the side, interested in striking up a conversation with Carly.

Misty paused for a few seconds, then answered, "Darla is putting her artistic eye to work in the house. It needs fresh paint and a few decorating tricks to rearrange the furniture."

Darla walked over to add more detail to the conversation. "I'm going to create a space that has Misty's personality. I have piles going to Goodwill, one for what Misty's keeping, and of course, there is a pile to be taken to a Dumpster." She batted her eyelashes with a grin. "Care to help?"

"I'll tell you what." He folded his arms across his chest and rocked back on his heels. "Misty can come with me, and I'll leave you Reese to help. He's at your service."

"Do you mind, Reese? Helping Carly and Darla while I go with Bronson?" Misty didn't want to force Reese into working in her home. After the roofing experience, he might have had enough.

Reese smiled a wicked grin at Carly. "Not at all. I'll be at these ladies' service."

"It's settled then." Bronson motioned toward the truck. "After you."

They climbed into the truck, and headed out. As they drove down the street, Misty panicked. They had been working on every room but the kitchen, and that was where she'd hidden her pre-natal vitamins and ultrasound pictures in the cabinet. She reached into her pocket, but her phone wasn't there. Darn, she'd left it home. All of a sudden, she had a sinking feeling they'd discover her secret sooner than she'd wanted. How could she warn Carly before it was too late?

Bronson drove into the parking lot of the fairgrounds, following the signs for vendor deliveries. Misty's mood changed from worried to excited, looking at all of the colorful booths and amusement rides.

"You seem pretty quiet. Something wrong?" He looked over at her with a warm smile.

"No. I'm fine." Positive she was overreacting, she dismissed her worry to concentrate on the sights before her. It was important to get a feel for the competition while they were making the delivery. She wanted to get glimpse of what she was up against. In four days, she would be going up against some of the top winning champions in the nation.

"Look, Misty, I know we had a deal about the supplies, but you don't have to worry. I've got it covered and you can keep all of the profits." He gave her a sideways glance. "I don't need you to pay me back."

His sweet gesture turned her insides into liquid butter. "I can't allow you to do that." She could use the extra funds, but her pride wouldn't allow her to accept his help. She didn't want Bronson to develop feelings out of some bizarre rescue syndrome. She'd worked hard to shed the handout reputation her mother had built up. It was bad enough he had helped her out as much as he had.

He pressed his foot on the brake, rolling to a complete stop. "Why not? I believe you have the best barbecue, and you can use the money you make from the fair to help fix up your home," he reasoned. It was a thoughtful gesture, but she wasn't his responsibility. She didn't know what they were to each other.

"I plan to win the prize money," she interjected. Squeezing out any doubts from her mind, she turned her attention back to the view of the fairgrounds.

He released his hold on the brake and pulled the trailer alongside a row of competitors. "Exactly, and you can take the prize money and the profits and fix your place up like your grandmother would have wanted."

Distracted, Misty read the sides of the professional trailers. *Bubba-Lou's—national champions four years in a row* was plastered along the side of one trailer, and Misty's hopes instantly sank. *Whisky Chick's Oak Smoked BBQ* had a huge custom trailer with a list of winning states was printed on the side in big bold letters.

"I didn't realize the competition would be this tough. There's no way my recipe on homemade equipment is going to win against these professionals." Her voice quivered. Tears began to form, and she tried to blink them away before he noticed.

Bronson pulled over again, placed the vehicle in park, and grabbed both of her hands in his. "Look at me."

She couldn't bring her eyes to meet this.

"Please," he said.

She shifted her gaze, studying his mouth as he began to speak. "They can spend all the money on the equipment and flash, but you have something they don't have. You put love into your food, and that's an ingredient they're all missing."

The sides of her mouth tugged into a smile. He believed in her; there was something in his voice that rang true.

"You also have the best grain-fed beef, pork, and chicken you can buy in this state because it's from my ranch," he boasted, giving her hands a squeeze. "You, sweetheart, are what they call a winner." He released her hands then lifted her chin with his finger before leaning in to place a gentle kiss on her lips. Drawing her closer, he shifted in his seat so he could kiss her a bit harder this time. A fire rose up in her, and she didn't want this kiss to end. All of the want, need, and loneliness within her overflowed. She fought the urge to run her hands over his chest. Instead, she moved her arms around his neck and pulled him closer.

A hard rap on the glass broke up the passionate kiss. Startled, they turned to see an older man wearing a neon orange vest, waving his arms for them to move, mouthing, "*You're blocking traffic.*"

Bronson signaled to the attendant that he understood, shifted into drive, and pulled into a parking spot. Misty placed a hand on her lips where they still burned from his kiss. Attempting to recover from their passionate kiss, Misty hurried to open the door and step out. "I'll go to the registration booth while you have our supplies inspected."

"Wait," he said, snatching her by the elbow. "We need to talk."

Her stomach dropped, and the intensity in his voice made her uncomfortable.

"I have something to tell you and something to ask you." The sun's rays streamed through the truck window creating a glow behind Bronson so that he looked mystical. Mesmerized by his handsome face, she waited for him to continue.

"Sit for a moment—please." His eyes pleaded with her. How could she refuse him? She climbed back in.

"Is it something important?" Misty was uncomfortable, confused, and wondering what couldn't wait until later. He looked at her, and the intensity of the glow behind him captured a magical moment.

Bronson was tired of pretending, living in denial, and fighting his attraction to Misty. He had created a long list of excuses as to why a relationship would never work with her, or anyone else for that matter. He glanced into the rearview mirror, perplexed by the stubborn man in the reflection. He looked like his mother, but the stubbornness in his eyes reminded him of his father. He turned his attention back to Misty.

"I've been trying to deny my feelings, but I'm pretty sure after that last kiss you know..." His voice trailed off. Every nerve ending tingled with excitement as he waited for a reply. He wanted her, and he hadn't felt feelings this strong—he didn't think—ever. He lifted her hand and gave it a kiss. She stared back at him in what looked like disbelief. "Do you feel the attraction?"

She smiled a weak smile, not what he was expecting. "Yes, I feel it too." That was all she said. He waited. Nothing else. Moments seemed like hours. It wasn't going as well as he would have liked. When she'd been at the ranch, they'd moved as if they were a perfect fit.

Laying it all on the line, he said, "I'd like us to—you know—start dating."

She looked at him as if he had two heads and was turning blue.

She studied him for a minute before she spoke. "If things were different maybe, but they're not. The timing's off. We want different things." She brushed a few stray hairs from around her eyes.

He almost thought he saw a tear in her eye, or was that wishful thinking. He wanted Misty in his life; could he make her understand they deserved a chance? "I can help you." He didn't understand why she was acting this way. "What are you afraid of? Getting hurt?" He understood that all too well. "I would never intentionally hurt you."

She wiggled back in her seat and looked out the front windshield. "I know. It's not you. It's me."

He cringed—not the line most guys used when breaking up with a woman. "If you don't have those type of feelings for me, say it now. Otherwise, give us a chance, and we can take it slow to see where it leads." She looked flustered, and he felt guilty for pressuring her.

"Can't we talk about this later? I need to check in and go over the cooking routine in my mind. Timing will be everything in this event."

She was right, and he was being selfish. He wasn't a cook and he didn't know what was involved—the mental preparation. This was the worst time to have a revelation about his feelings. When it came to women, timing had never been his thing. For now, this conversation was over.

"You're right." He nodded, more to himself than her, then opened his truck door. "We can talk about this later." Next time, he'd make damn sure he changed her mind.

Painted walls of dove gray, creamy shades of white, and pale seafoam green were now everywhere Misty looked as she walked through the transformed rooms. Darla had done an amazing job with a little paint and rearranging of the furniture over the last few days while Misty prepared for the competition. Bronson supervised Levi as he constructed her booth for the fair; all of the nonperishable supplies had been delivered and stored. As soon as the committee allowed Bronson to the deliver the meats for the event, she would begin the smoking process.

For the first time since she'd arrived in Crystal Cove, she felt like this was really her home. She walked into the spare bedroom—soon to be her baby's. She imagined bringing her baby home from the hospital to a beautifully decorated nursery. Only Carly knew that this bedroom was designated the baby's room. A few times, she'd almost slipped and referred to it as the nursery in front of Darla, but quickly recovered by calling it another guest bedroom.

She thought about Bronson. He wanted a relationship; she wanted one too. She hadn't given him an answer yet. In a way, she had hoped he would change his mind. She didn't want to look into his eyes and see hurt, pain, or disappointment when he learned of her situation. Bronson had even offered her Jim's position since Jim said he'd be leaving soon, but she wasn't sure if she wanted to be attached to the McCabe brothers at all.

Once they found out about this baby, they might question who the father was, and she wasn't prepared to answer. The rodeo circuit was a close-knit family, and all four of the McCabe men had connections too it. What was worse, Beau was well known and financially well off. What if he wanted visitation rights? Or—what if he felt he could give their child a better home? He could seek full custody, and that wasn't a risk she was willing to take.

Outside, she heard the crunch of gravel as if someone had pulled into the driveway. It was too soon for Carly and Darla to have returned from their errands. They had left to drop off more donation items to Goodwill and then stop by Darla's to pick up a few things she was giving Misty for the house. Darla had a surplus of furnishings over at her place; she said a few pieces would fit perfectly at Misty's. She finished straightening the comforter on the bed, then hurried downstairs, not surprised when she heard Bronson's familiar rap on the door. His showing up unannounced left her a little on edge.

Opening the door, she said, "I'm surprised to see you here today." Her eyes moved over his hard chest, down his body, and back up again to the smile he wore.

"I came to get my answer. Do you have one for me yet?" He stepped inside and closed the door. He stood so close to her every cell in her body screamed to touch him.

She was in a weakened state around him, all senses lost and the only emotions were lust and love. He wanted her answer about a relationship, and she wanted to say no, but heard a "Yes" escape her lips.

"Does that mean yes you have an answer or yes you want to try a relationship?"

She nodded and leaned in closer. Instinctively, he dipped

his head down and placed a firm kiss on her lips. His lips were soft, warm, and he smelled like musk. She placed her arms around him, and he wrapped her in a hard embrace. He trailed kisses down her neck, searing her skin. Her head swirled with thoughts to push him away. Stop. Without complete honesty, his passion was a lie. She had to tell him, but how? Not wanting his touch to end, she stayed where she was. She would tell him after the fair.

The doorbell rang, and they jumped, breaking the magic of the moment. Now what? She pressed a hand on his chest and pushed off to be free from his grasp to answer the door.

Before she could open it, she heard Arlene yell, "Misty, it's me. I have news about the competition." Arlene let herself in before Misty had a chance to, and when her gaze landed on Bronson, her eyebrows lifted in surprise. "Sorry if I'm interrupting," Arlene murmured, then turned her attention back to Misty.

"Two men came in the cafe this morning, for breakfast. While I was chatting with them, they started asking about you. By the line of questioning, they were looking for something."

"Me? What did they say?"

"They were wondering how long you'd worked for me. I explained you didn't, you supplied meals on occasion.

One was tall and lean. The other was short and stocky. I asked the tall lanky one why he wanted to know." She frowned, pressing her lips together. "He said he liked good barbecue and heard yours was the best around. Different. He wanted to know if I knew what was in it—what made it unique." Arlene rolled her eyes. "Musta thought I was born yesterday if he thought I would give out that information."

Bronson stood with his arms folded across his chest, taking it all in. "Sounds like Bubba and Lou. They probably heard they have real competition this year. They're trying to secure another win. Rumor is they have a tendency to find out the key ingredients of the competition and outdo their rivals."

"There's no chance of that happening. My recipe is all up here," Misty said, tapping a finger on the side of her head. She had a few key secret ingredients, spices, and brand-named products when it came to the pineapple and core ingredients. Over the years, she'd heard certain products had richer flavors. She didn't buy top shelf brands; instead, she chose by flavor. The real key was cooking it over the stove and letting it sit so the flavors of the sauce married—a cooking term she'd learned on television.

She needed to win this competition. She'd have to deal with Bronson and her feelings for him later. If Bubba and Lou wanted to outdo her, let them try. This prize money would secure her baby's future, and if she was lucky, help launch her product line of Summer Heat sauces.

"If Bubba and Lou think they can cheat their way to the top, they're sadly mistaken. If its competition they want, I'll bring it."

B ronson had volunteered to keep watch overnight. He looked exhausted and Misty felt guilty she'd had the good night's sleep he lacked. Hard work from the preparations the day before had her passing out right after dinner.

The meat had to be delivered and inspected two days before the competition, no pre-seasoned or injected marinades were allowed until after the inspection and must be made on site. The Florida Barbecue Society stored all the meats in a locked refrigerator and posted a guard until the competition began. The rules were very strict, and Misty couldn't have done any of this without the help of the town.

"I can't believe Bronson stayed here all night. If that's not love, I don't know what is," Carly whispered in

Misty's ear.

"I didn't think it was necessary but he insisted," she replied while basting another rack of ribs. The thick sauce flavored with sweetness and heat had a line of people wrapped several times around her booth.

All the planning in the world hadn't prepared Misty for the amount of foot traffic stopping at her booth to taste her secret recipe. It had been years since she's attended the fair as a child. Her memory had dulled over time and the hungry crowd had multiplied. Levi had built her an amazing booth; it resembled a real storefront. Compared to the other professionals who had custom trailers, Misty's booth had a homey feel with shingles, stone, and even a little mailbox—Darla's idea—hung on the side for comments and suggestions.

Everyone wore the Summer Heat T-shirts designed by Darla. Misty felt a little ridiculous dressed in yellow, with orange and red flames licking the lower part of the shirt body. She had to hand it to Darla; the design did work to draw the people in. More than one customer had commented they'd love to buy one of the shirts.

Arlene had organized the Summer Heat support team, and they were working the crowd, directing them to Misty's booth and making sure they voted—with any luck they'd select Summer Heat as their favorite and she'd win the crowd favorite award. She'd started smoking the meat before dawn, and Misty hadn't had any coffee because of her pregnancy. She'd decided to cut it out as much as possible, but with the excitement causing her adrenaline to flow, she didn't need the caffeine today.

Bronson, Braxton, Radford, and Reese all worked various stages of the smokers. Lifting the slabs of beef, pork, roasts, and chicken from the refrigeration area onto a cart bringing them over to the smoker. The intense heat made it important to stay hydrated; Arlene took charge, appointing a beverage runner who made sure everyone manning the smokers or on the support team had a full glass at all times. From a small idea, it had all come together.

Misty hadn't eaten a bite since she'd nibbled on a piece of toast just before dawn. Now, half past noon, she was beginning to feel lightheaded. She didn't know how much longer she could last without a break to eat. Heat of the day, hot coals, and the smell of barbecue caused her to be dizzy, hungry, and nauseous all at the same time. Nausea won out. Bringing the back of her hand up to her forehead, she dabbed the cold beads of sweat.

"Carly, take over for me." Removing her apron and tossing it on a small ledge next to the counter, Misty walked on wobbly legs to a nearby chair. She hoped a few moments of rest and a cool glass of lemonade would help settle her stomach.

She felt a firm hand on her back. "Are you all right?" Bronson asked. "What's wrong?" He walked around and stood in front of her, concern riddled his weary face.

"I'll be fine. Nothing that a cold glass of lemonade can't fix." She forced a weak smile. "Maybe something to eat would help once my stomach has settled."

"Girl, what the heck's wrong with you? You're green." Arlene pushed past Bronson to muscle her way in.

"I'll be fine. I've been pushing myself a lot lately with the house and the fair. The heat got to be too much on an empty stomach." Empty pregnant stomach she wanted to say, but remained silent.

Arlene turned to walk back over to where the food was being assembled for the customers' orders. "Well, let me correct that right now."

Misty made a feeble attempt to argue. "Arlene, wait. I'm not sure I…"

Bronson bent down and looked her in the eye. "She's right. You do have a green hue." He stood. "I'll be right back." He walked over to the ice bin and filled a small towel with ice, then returned to place it on her forehead.

Reaching to remove it, she said, "Oh, it's cold."

Bronson held it in place. "Leave it on for a few minutes." He waited, not allowing her the chance take it off, then moved it to the back of her neck after a bit.

"Sorry I took so long." Arlene returned with a nice

assortment of food, but Misty couldn't stomach much more than the plain roll. "Haven't seen too many people turn green before. Once on a fishing boat and another when—"

"Thanks. I'm in no hurry to eat," she snapped, cutting Arlene off, hoping the woman didn't make the connection. She broke off a small piece of the bread. "I really need to get back to work." She started to get up, but Bronson pushed her back into the chair.

"You've been going nonstop for days. We've got it covered. Relax and breathe."

Misty took a few deep breaths in an attempt to calm down. "I do have a tendency to hold my breath when I'm stressed—bad habit."

Arlene remained silent and arched an eyebrow.

Braxton hollered for Bronson.

"Be right back," he said before he went to offer his brother a hand.

Arlene watched him leave then snapped her attention back to Misty, eyeing her suspiciously. "So how long have you felt this way?"

Misty flushed. Arlene was fishing for information. "All of today." Which was not a lie. Her morning sickness had passed a while ago. This was a simple case of being overworked, hot, and not eating enough. *And pregnant.*

Arlene placed her hand on Misty's arm. "If you need to talk, I'm always here." She glanced over to the booth, then yelled at one of the support team members to stop slacking and headed in that direction. Misty sat there in the middle of a crowded fair but she had never felt so alone. At least she had Carly for support when everyone found out her secret and her heart broke.

The judging started in exactly one hour. Misty took a few more bites from the roll, pressed the ice on the back of her neck, and downed the rest of the sugary lemon mixture. It was just what she'd needed to settle her stomach. Blowing out a long breath, she stood and stretched. This was it. Weeks of testing and preparing to take home the prize money.

Would her family recipe stand up against the champion-winning professionals—Bubba-Lou's and Whisky Chicks? Or maybe another competitor would pull off a win. She would know by the end of today. It was time to stop wondering and to prepare her trays for the judge's table. Misty was grateful for all of the support she was getting. If it weren't for Bronson and his brothers, Arlene, Carly, Levi, Darla, and the team Arlene pulled together, she never would have been able to accomplish it.

Darla had looked up food-styling online two nights ago at her home. Neither Misty nor Carly had known there was such a thing. After viewing a list of online tutorials, Darla suggested subtle ways to make Misty's dishes visually appealing to the judges. Taste scored the majority of the points, but Misty needed every advantage if she was going to win this year. After the judging, the winners would be announced at a closing ceremony. Butterflies fluttered in her stomach at the thought. Did she dare to dream? The prize money would help her take care of her baby, and she could begin her product line. The thought of standing on her own without the help of anyone would be a dream come true.

"You feeling better?" Carly asked.

Arlene commented, "At least she's not green anymore."

Darla pulled out the required trays to take to the judging table. "I don't blame you for feeling ill; we've been in a steam oven for hours here. The stress has me on the verge of collapse, and I'm not even in the completion."

"Thank you all for being here and for all of the help." Misty looked over to the men at the smokers. "Hey, guys, can you bring some of the finished ribs, pork, and brisket this way. We should taste portions of the meats and see which ones rate the highest. Those will be the ones chosen to be placed on the judging trays."

Radford picked up a metal baking sheet. "On my way."

Bronson, Braxton, and Reese followed. After the group tasted, voted, and styled the platters, it was time to fill the trays with food and take them over to the judging table.

Misty, Bronson, Darla, Arlene, and Carly all carried them over. Once placed on the table, Misty remained in the judging tent, her heart pounding so hard she was sure the judges sitting across from her could see it beating out of her chest.

Bronson leaned down to whisper in her ear. "Remember, you're gonna win. Your key ingredient is love." He gave her hand a squeeze, and like the rest of her friends, he was gone.

After a long day of waiting, the winners were about to be announced. Some of the crowd was getting rowdy and impatient after a heavy day of hard work and beer drinking. Misty, the McCabe brothers, Carly, Darla, Arlene, and the rest of the support team moved closer to the center stage where the president of the Florida Barbecue Society would announce the runners-up and the winner of the ten thousand dollar prize.

Misty marveled at the turnout. If anything, she'd gained confidence from the experience, and the amount of exposure could only help her recipe catch on. Someone announced this year that they'd anticipated over five hundred thousand people to attend over the course of the twelve days the fair was open. Thankfully, she hadn't had to work all twelve days.

Misty couldn't shake the hopeful feeling that she'd won. She had a severe case of the jitters, and her stomach flopped while the president spoke to the crowd about the history of barbecue. Her mind drifted, imagining she was walking up onto the stage, receiving the check that would change her life, positive from the amount of customers who'd said they would vote for her that she'd have enough to win the crowd favorite award.

Carly wrapped an arm around Misty and gave her a quick hug for good luck. "I wish he'd go ahead and make the announcement already," she said loud enough for the people around them to hear, and several men nodded in agreement.

"I know right," Darla said sarcastically. "He says the same piece on barbecue history every year. Doesn't this guy have anything better to talk about?"

From where she stood, Misty could see the Whisky Chicks' and Bubba-Lou's large crowds of supporters waving signs; they cheered whenever the word barbecue was announced into the microphone, heightening her nervous tension.

As the president started to broadcast the winners, the crowd cheered so loud Misty couldn't understand the announcer's words. They started with a lesser prize, but it would have made things easier if he'd asked the crowd to control their enthusiasm until they announced all the winners over the loudspeaker.

"The first category is chicken. Let's see who the lucky recipient is of this beautiful trophy." The zealous voice squealed through the overhead speaker. A state fair representative held up a shiny gold trophy while the president opened the envelope. "Our third runner-up— winner of a one thousand dollar prize package…"

As he went through the other categories, he proceeded to read off the prize winners for pork butt, brisket, and was about to give out the prize for ribs, but all Misty wanted to hear was who'd won the overall grand prize. Finally, the time came to announce the overall top three winners, one of which would win the grand prize.

"Get ready to welcome our third runner-up. Give a round of applause for the Whiskey Chicks." Deafening cheers and screams erupted. "I know that many of you enjoyed their food."

"Second runner-up, with sweet and savory racks of barbecue—meat so tender it fell off the bone, and I know because I had several myself," he joked.

Misty held her breath, hoping her name wasn't called until he said grand prize champion.

"And the winner is…Misty Summers, with her sweet and tangy, steamy blend of sweet heat, a perfect blend called

Summer Heat."

Misty's entire body went weak; those high hopes pulverized by the loss. The crowd cheered, and a mixture of pride and disappointment showed on the faces of her team. Everyone had worked so hard. With shaky legs, she made her way to the stage, fighting the urge flee. She should be grateful to have placed among the finalists, but she'd wanted more. She'd needed this win. It had been a long shot, but dreams did come true, so why couldn't it be her turn?

Once she'd made her way to the stage, the president declared at full volume, "The grand prize winner, of the ten thousand dollar prize is...Bubba-Lou's!"

The lanky and stocky cowboy duo raced up onto the stage amid the roars of the crowd. Misty's mind scanned over her list of hopes that now evaporated into thin air. The meager second-place prize money of two thousand dollars, would do little in comparison to winning the grand prize. It would be a help with the baby, but not enough to finish the repairs on the house or take care of the taxes.

"On behalf of the Florida Barbecue Society, I'd like to congratulate all the winners," the president continued. Forcing a fake smile, she accepted her check, hurried to the stairs, and dashed in the opposite direction of the crowd. Misty was desperate to avoid facing the people she loved; they'd worked so hard to support her dream, but more important in her heart, the opportunity to honor her grandmother's memory was lost.

The midmorning sun peeked through the kitchen window, blinding Misty while she gazed at the ultrasound image again for the dozenth time in the past hour.

"Don't let this get you down. You were a finalist," Carly consoled. "I tasted Bubba-Lou's, and I don't understand what all the hoopla was about."

Misty gasped. "You ate the competition's food?" The agony of yesterday's defeat was still raw. She propped her baby's image against the salt and pepper shakers where she could see it at a glance.

Carly reached across the table for the sugar and poured two teaspoons into her coffee. "Something about it appealed to the judges. Damn if I know." Her spoon clanged in her coffee mug while she gave it a slow stir.

"I guess." Her wounded pride sparked insecurities. It reminded her that to be number one in Crystal Cove meant she was a big fish in a small pond, or in this case, the lone fish a small bowl. "I've gotta figure out what I'm going to fix with this money. I guess scratch off the new nursery furniture." She'd have to buy used furniture at a thrift center or garage sale.

Misty snapped her head around when the smell of something burning hit her nostrils. The toaster had jammed. Out of it, a puff of black smoke floated toward the ceiling. Rushing to pull the plug out of the wall, she frowned and said, "Add a cheap toaster instead." The old hunk of metal, which looked like it had been nursed along for years, had finally given out.

Carly looked unfazed and took a sip from her cup. "What did Bronson say?"

Misty shrugged. "Not much. That I didn't have to pay him back for the supplies."

"That's not what I meant and you know it," Carly snapped, rolling her eyes.

"I don't understand what you're asking." She did not want to discuss it today.

"Ugh, hello—about the two of you having a relationship!"

Misty rubbed her forehead to forestall the headache she was sure would develop over this topic. "I don't know how to tell him about the baby."

Carly stood up, walked over to the coffee pot, and poured another cup. "You have to. He's going to find out, and you need to tell him before it's gone too far."

"It already has." Misty scraped off the blackened section of the bread with a knife over the sink. She didn't mind it a little well done, but the burnt taste added to her sour mood.

"If he loves you, he'll understand."

Misty spun around. "Really? Would you understand?" Could she accept it if Bronson was about to become a father, another woman carrying his child, would she accept the woman's child? There was an awkward silence. "See what I mean. You couldn't overlook it. How can I expect him to?"

"I'd have to think about it." Carly downed the last few drops from her mug. "I have to get ready. I have a lunch date."

It wasn't even ten yet. "With who?" Misty wondered why Carly would be leaving this early when half of the Crystal Cove shops weren't open yet.

"Darla and I have a fun day planned. I'll call you on my way back." Carly placed her cup in the sink and started toward her bedroom.

Misty called after her. "Why wasn't I invited for the fun?" Not that she really wanted to go anywhere. She needed to rest after yesterday. She was surprised Carly and Darla had the energy to go anywhere. They'd both worked so hard all week leading up to last night.

Carly yelled back, "I thought you'd be too tired—you know."

Misty understood, and the truth was she didn't have the desire to go anywhere. She'd rather be alone today after yesterday's utter disappointment. She wasn't going to answer the phone and hoped no one showed up at the door.

"Have a good time. I'm going upstairs to take a shower." Then maybe read or try to knit or crochet. She had the entire day to kick back and relax…and to work out her problems. Somehow she had to figure out a way to tell Bronson she was carrying another man's child.

Debra Fisk

Things needed to be said. Words needed to be spoken. All the waiting was driving Bronson crazy. Patience wasn't his best trait. He didn't like beating around a subject. He preferred the direct approach. He stood on Misty's front porch, about to ring the bell, when the door opened.

Carly looked at him, surprised. "Oh, hey, Bronson. Is Misty expecting you?" She was dressed up, and it looked to him like they were about to go out.

"Uh, no, she isn't. I guess I came over at a bad time. It looks like you ladies are going out."

"I am. Darla's picking me up, and we're going out for the day. Misty's in the shower. Why don't you go inside, have a cup of coffee, and wait until she's out?" She held open the door for him, and he stepped inside, just as Darla pulled into the driveway.

"Nice seeing you. Tell Misty I won't be home until tonight." Carly smirked, giving him a wink. "So you two can work things out," she said before leaving rather hastily.

"Thanks."

She giggled as she pulled the door shut behind her. At least someone was on his side; maybe he could talk some sense into Misty now that they would be alone. He walked into the kitchen to help himself to that cup of coffee. The smell of burnt toast hung in the air; he surmised what had happened once he spied the charred metal toaster on the counter. He poured a cup of coffee and took a seat at the table, thinking about how he was going convince Misty they were meant to be together, and to at least try to see where it might lead. His eyes panned the kitchen. He couldn't believe the transformation a little cleanup and paint had done to her home. His eyes rested on a photo propped up on the table.

In the corner of the picture, it read Baby Summers-Misty Summers with a date and measurement. He stared at it, scanning the details; his teeth clenched and every vein in his body pulsed from the adrenaline rush. Misty was pregnant? His stomach clenched like he'd been punched in the gut.

That couldn't be. Who was the father? Looking at the date, he did the calculations. She had been pregnant when she'd arrived in Crystal Cove. All this time she was cuddling up to him and she was carrying another man's child. Sickened by how easily he'd been made a fool. The anger, hurt, and disgust infuriated him. He had to leave—get out—get away from her before she claimed innocence with her creative lies. She was a master manipulator compared to her mother.

The soft footsteps padded down the stairs, before Misty came into the kitchen. "Bronson, what are you—"

Shock and horror etched hard lines in Misty's face when she realized what he was holding in his hand. The side of his jaw ticced.

"Carly let me in," he ground out. He charged toward her.

"I was going to tell you. Let me explain," she pleaded, taking a step backward. Tears formed in her eyes, but they couldn't penetrate his hardened heart this time.

"When! When were you going to tell me, because I would really like to know." He tossed the picture on the table. "Who's the father? Do you even know?" She flinched as if she'd been struck by his words. He regretted the last part of his statement. How could he have been so wrong about her? Pain and anger took over; all of the hurt and embarrassment from Delilah bubbled to the surface. It was as if he was reliving one of the worst moments of his life while standing in front of Misty.

Her expression changed from hurt to anger. "Of course I know. It's none of your business." She snatched the picture off the table. "You have your opinion of me, but for your information, I'm nothing like my mother. This baby comes first." She clenched her fists and shook from the emotion. "I don't suppose you have ever made a mistake in your life."

He had, plenty, especially over the years with his brothers and the ranch. He searched his memory for something of this magnitude but came up short. He wanted to understand, yet he couldn't overcome the hurt and disappointment long enough to calm down and speak rationally.

"Well, I'm not perfect like you," she sneered. "I have made mistakes—at least I am taking responsibility for my child. I'm not looking for handouts. I had hoped to win the prize money. It would have made my life a heck of a lot easier."

It sure would have. "Especially when you had me fronting you all of the supplies for free. Relying on a contest win for your future wasn't a great plan."

"I offered to pay you back," she murmured. Hurt showed in her eyes.

He hated to ask, but he had to. "Does anyone else know

about the baby?" He wondered if Doc Harrison knew or Darla. Was he the town joke again?

She frowned. "Carly." Misty pulled out a chair and took a seat, looking worn out from their heated exchange. "I wanted to tell you and had planned on it. I just didn't know how. The baby's father doesn't know." She sighed.

What type of man was she involved with where she didn't feel comfortable telling him she was pregnant?

"Were you two in a relationship?" Bronson fought the desire to know every detail; he tried to make sense of what had just happened. This wasn't how he'd pictured this day going. Any thoughts of a relationship or future together was now lost.

"It wasn't like that," she explained. "I had a lapse in judgment. Not something I do often. It happened and I'm dealing with it." She looked relieved, like she was tired of keeping her secret. She looked up at him, and a he wanted to believe what she was saying. Could she even fathom how much it hurt to learn about her pregnancy like this?

"Are you going to tell the baby's father?" Not that it should matter to him one way to the other. He really needed to leave, the pain of her betrayal hurt too much. He was too big to cry, and so angry he wanted to punch a hole in the wall. With his jaw clenched, he struggled to maintain control until he had all the answers to his questions.

She shook her head. "I hadn't planned on it." Rubbing her temple, she blew out a long breath. "Then part of me understands he has the right to know. To tell the truth, I'm afraid to tell him. He's a bull rider, travels the rodeo circuit, and has enough money to obtain a lawyer to seek paternity rights if he wants to."

So, she had an affair with some rich cowboy and wound up carrying his child. Was she telling the truth? Maybe Misty had already told the guy and he had his reasons to abandon the situation? He wasn't sure what to think.

"Then I guess you have a lot to think about." Now that he had all of the answers he needed, he was at a loss for words. So he did the only thing he knew how: tipped his hat and walked out the door.

Bronson pulled away from Misty's house without so much as a glance in the rearview mirror. He had driven halfway to the ranch when his cell phone rang. He ignored it, not wanting to speak to anyone for a while.

When it rang for the third time, he glanced over at the screen. *Radford.* Guilt settled in. What if something was wrong or a worker had been injured? He had to take the call, but with his mind still unfocused by his visit with Misty, he pulled over and parked. It had to be serious if his brother called him three times.

"Rad, what is it?" he barked, taking out his frustration on his brother.

"Sorry to bother. Are you at the Summers place?" Rad asked.

"Is that why you called?" He was about to disconnect, but Rad rambled on and something caught his attention. He thought he heard Rad mention the fair. "What did you say?"

"I said it's a huge scandal. Bubba and Lou were caught cheating!" Rad exclaimed so loud Bronson had to pull the phone away from his ear. "They used professional marinades and injected it into the meats. They didn't make their own barbecue sauce either," he added.

"I don't understand how they got those supplies past the inspectors," Bronson said. Why did he even care? He and Misty were through; he had to try to remember that. Bronson had an itch to hang up and call Misty; instead, he listened as Rad explained.

"They rebottled the professional products into their own containers. Two of Bubba and Lou's workers came forward and produced proof when Bubba and Lou decided to cheat them out of their share of the prize money they were promised.

"There's a huge investigation. The fair commissioner and the president of the Florida Barbecue Society are holding on meeting on how to proceed. They could even prosecute."

Bronson wasn't sure if the last part was true. "They should have to return the prize money." His heart ached. Yesterday, he was excited, in love, and actually felt bad for Misty when she'd lost. Now, the dreams he'd had for their future were shattered, his life completely flipped. He'd lost at love again, and it ripped open the old wounds, the death of his parents, then Delilah, and the so-called close friend she'd run off with. If this weren't a sign he should remain a loner, what was?

"You do realized this makes Misty the real winner."

"I suppose it does. Good for her." And he meant it. She deserved the prize money; she'd worked hard and should have won.

"Are you going to tell her?"

"Why don't you call her and tell her? I'm kinda tied up right now." It was a lie but he didn't want to talk to her. "I'm not with her, and she deserves to know right away."

"Oh, okay. Where are you?"

"I gotta go…" He hung up and sat in the truck, thinking about the shocking events of the last hour. His world had changed. He'd changed inside, and he would never be the same again.

Misty heard the front door close and Bronson's truck rumble down the driveway. She placed her head in her hands and began to sob. All of the pain and heartache from her mother, the pregnancy, her grandmother's death, and the contest came pouring out in a river of tears. Coming to Crystal Cove had been a mistake.

She couldn't bear living in this town and not be part of Bronson's life. She had to get away, to think, clear her head, and figure out a new plan for her future.

She picked up her cell phone and tried to call Arlene. After several attempts to place the call, it went straight to voicemail so she left an urgent message. Then she tried to contact Carly. It rang and rang. Misty sighed. She must be out of range. For some reason, the front porch had the best signal for her cell phone. She opened the door to go outside in an attempt to get better reception.

It was time for her to contact Beau. He had a right to know about their baby. Even if he didn't want to be a part of Misty's life, he might want to be part of their baby's.

Of all the people she had tried to call, Beau was the one who picked up on the first ring.

With a shaky voice, she said, "Hey, Beau, it's me. Misty. How ya been?" She'd read he was doing very well, and she was happy for him. It was time to visit him so they could talk. "Saw you on the cover of Rodeo Circuit Magazine. It said you live in Citrus County. Are you still there?"

"I sure am." He sounded happy to hear from her. Maybe she'd been wrong in her thinking.

"I moved to Florida. I live a few towns away." It would be better if she could talk to him in person.

"You do? Well why don't you visit me?"

Perfect, that would give her the chance to tell him about the baby. She was tired of hiding the fact she was pregnant.

"Sounds great. I'll let you know when I'm leaving."

"I'll wait right here," he said. "Drive carefully." That was sweet of him.

She hung up her cell phone right as Arlene pulled into the driveway. She hurried out of her car and asked, "What's the emergency? I rushed right here."

Misty flopped into the porch swing, and the well of tears opened up again. "Bronson and I had a horrible fight." Misty explained through heavy sobs—about Beau, her pregnancy, and what had happened—and hoped Arlene could understand enough as she forced the words out.

"Please don't judge me, Arlene. I was doing what I thought was best."

Arlene grabbed Misty's hand. "Honey, I surmised you were pregnant when you turned green. I didn't want to pry. I figured you would tell me when you were ready." Arlene's voice sounded gentle and loving. "To tell you the truth, I thought you were pregnant by Bronson. I'm sorry about what happened. Things are still too raw for him. Give him time." Arlene placed the keys into Misty's hand. "Go ahead and take my car. I hope you find the happiness you deserve."

Misty threw her arms around Arlene and placed a kiss on her cheek. "Thank you so very much," she said. "Once I speak with Beau, I'll call you and bring your car back."

"No need to thank me. That's what friends are for," she stated.

They went inside, and Arlene marveled at the picture of baby Summers. Misty picked up a pad from the kitchen counter, flipped over the grocery list, and began writing Carly a note explaining what had happened.

Misty gave the older woman a hug. "I promise to be careful with the car." It was time to pack her things and move on. She needed a break and maybe even start a life with Beau.

Debra Fisk

"Under the circumstances, I think it's best if you marry me."

Misty stared at Beau Carson, waiting for the punch line. Was this a joke? The way he stated it so matter-of-factly puzzled her. What was Beau thinking? She couldn't marry him based on her condition. His handsome face was serious; his expression unchanged. They sat together on the front porch of his brand-new home, looking out as his horses grazed in the open terrain. Spending two days together wasn't enough to make a lifelong decision.

"I don't want my child to grow up without a father. I was raised to do the right thing and take responsibility for my actions." Beau came from the picture perfect all-America type of family, completely different from Misty's background. Sadness filled her heart at the memory of what it had been like growing up without a father. Her confused and misdirected mother hadn't been ready to be a parent when she'd become pregnant, and Misty had paid the price.

Misty looked at Beau. She certainly didn't want him to live with regrets. "We can talk about this later." She hoped to table that part of the conversation until he had more time to digest the news.

He furrowed his brow. "What's to talk about? You wanted me to be part of this baby's life. That's why you're here, isn't it?"

Yes. No. Maybe? Why was she there? How could she explain it without sounding harsh?

She tried a different approach. "Usually people get married because they love each other, then decide to raise a family." She took a sip of water from her glass. "I'm here because you have a right to know. I hadn't thought much past that." It was true. She hadn't, and now Misty realized she might have made another bad decision by involving Beau. His impulsive action might cause her grief in the future.

"I'm glad you told me. To tell you the truth, I've thought about settling down. I built this new home with that thought in mind. Maybe it's fate, you showing up here." His rugged features, white smile, and boyish charm could work their magic and make a girl say yes. She could do a lot worse—much worse.

A small, microscopic part of her held out hope somehow Bronson would change his mind, but that ship had sailed and sunk. She'd study the situation and then decide what would be best for this baby. There was no reason to jump at Beau's proposal. Besides, he might change his mind after a day or two. If they could get along and seemed compatible, she'd consider marriage.

"I'll stay a few days as a test to see how we get along, to learn more about one another. After a few days' time, we can reevaluate the situation and see if this is something we both want."

"Agreed. I'm going to go tend to the horses. Make yourself at home till I get back." Beau stood, giving her a wide grin. "Got a rodeo this weekend, and I'm aiming to win it all." He winked and then jumped down the steps. Misty watched him jog toward the lavish stables that were built better than most homes.

She had to call Carly, who'd already left several messages, but Misty had ignored them, refusing to listen until she'd had time to speak with Beau and work a few things out in her head.

Dialing Carly's number, she heard her pick it up on the first ring. "Misty, where are you? What's going on? It's been two days. Why haven't you called? All you did was leave me a crazy message—*'Bronson found out'*—then disappeared. I had to get all the details from Arlene!"

"I'm here with Beau, at his house in Citrus County." It could be their house if she decided to marry him. The huge ranch with a large wraparound porch and endless fields would be a beautiful place to raise a child. She paused long enough to toy with the idea to tell Carly about Beau's proposal.

"Sorry about Bronson, but I have big news. You won the fair! The ten thousand dollars—it's yours." Carly shrieked so loud Misty had to switch ears, positive that her eardrum had suffered some type of damage.

Confused, she asked, "What do you mean? The fair's over and I lost." She hadn't thought about it since she'd arrived at Beau's ranch.

Carly began to speak quickly. "Bubba-Lou's cheated. They used bottled sauces and marinades. It's become a big scandal, and you're missing all the action. You need to come back." Carly stopped to catch a breath. "The Barbecue Society declared you the winner. You can pick up your check at any time. It's on the front page of the town newspaper."

Had she heard Carly correctly? Was she dreaming? Winning the prize money would enable her to start her own business and buy all the needed baby items.

She leaned back in the porch swing. "I don't know what to say. I'm in shock."

"How fast can you be back?"

"In a few days, Beau and I have to work some things out." Misty avoided bringing up the subject of Bronson. It was the sole reason she hesitated to drive back home right now. She might be able to steer clear of him for a few days, but eventually they would cross paths.

"How did Beau react?"

Different. Kind. Considerate.

"Calm. Unusually calm. Not what I had expected." She decided not to hold back the rest of the information. "He's offered to marry me."

"Get out! Girl, you'll be the envy of every young woman in America." Carly wasn't wrong. Beau had a huge fan base from tweens to middle-aged women who'd love to become Mrs. Carson.

"I haven't said yes." And she doubted she would, but maybe they could work an arrangement out that didn't include marriage.

Her best friend called her out. "I can tell you're thinking about it by the tone of your voice." Carly knew her all too well.

"I'd be a fool not to. His offer is genuine. Although, for the life of me, I can't figure out why he'd want to get married even though we're having the baby."

"Stop it. A man would be crazy not to want you for a wife."

Misty's hopes slumped. "Bronson didn't." It was what she'd expected, yet it hurt more than she'd imagined.

"Bronson's proud. He'll come around—eventually," Carly assured her.

If only that were true. As each day passed, her dream of a future with Bronson would slip farther away.

The only peace Bronson could find over the last few days was riding his horse. Alone. Stopping to give his horse a drink, he looked out at the open terrain. If only he could clear out his frustration. He wanted to be free of his feelings for Misty. He'd avoided his brothers, refrained from going into town, even from answering his cell phone. His last conversation had been with Carly when she had shown up on his doorstep after Misty left town. Carly had filled him in on the details of Misty's situation, but it didn't erase the fact that she'd deceived him. Did she expect him to overlook another man's child?

Bronson ground his teeth. Right now, Misty was spending time with the baby's father. If she had expectations of building a life with a man she spent one night with, she was sadly mistaken. He probably hadn't given Misty a second thought in months. Didn't she understand?

He growled in annoyance. His sole purpose for minimal human contact these last few days has been to steer clear of conversations about her, and here he was thinking about her. Ever since the barbecue scandal news broke, he knew he couldn't go anywhere without her name coming up. This salacious piece of information would have the townspeople talking like never before.

How much of the town knew Misty was pregnant? Arlene and Carly, for starters. That was enough to fuel the town gossip, but he hadn't heard anyone mention it in the brief contact he had outside of the ranch. He heard a horse galloping up behind him. Shielding his eyes from the sun, he saw Jim atop his tall chestnut mare. Bronson had a pretty good idea why Jim had saddled his horse and ridden out to find him.

"I thought you could use some company. Wanna talk?" Jim pulled his horse alongside Bronson's and dismounted.

Not really. Did he have a choice? Bronson shrugged. "Sure."

"You—better than anyone—realize life can throw some pretty mean curve balls—with losing both your parents." Jim paused to clear his throat. "I'm sorry I'm moving out and I understand how you think. I'm not abandoning you and your brothers. You boys mean the world to me, like the sons I never had. I missed out on a lot in life; a wife —family of my own. By my choices. Didn't think I needed love. I didn't want to compromise my ways— give up my freedom. I thought I had it all figured out. I didn't need anyone." Jim pushed back his hat and looked Bronson right in the eye. "Life's giving me a second chance at love. Something I missed and didn't think I needed."

Bronson grew a bit emotional. "If I haven't said it lately, thank you for the years you've devoted to our family. I understand, and believe me, I don't fault you."

Jim's eyes grew moist. "I appreciate that, but I'm telling you this so you'll understand. Do you love this girl... Misty?"

Bronson didn't want to talk about it. Not with Jim—not anyone. When Misty deceived him, she slammed the door on any chance for a future they might have had together. "That's not the issue. You don't know—it's complicated." His voice broke with emotion. "This situation's completely different. There's more to it."

Jim shook his head and frowned. "Your brothers told me. If the situation involved the two of you and nothing else, would you love her enough to marry her—to be happy?"

It was easy for Jim to shell out advice when he'd lived a

completely different type of life.

Jim pressed him for an answer. "Do you love her?"

The hair on the back of Bronson's neck stood on end as he realized the truth. "Yes." And no amount of solitary time on his ranch would change his answer.

Jim tapped Bronson on the chest with an index finger. "Then go find Misty and tell her. Don't make the mistakes I did and miss out on a life of happiness. You might not get a second chance."

Jim was right. Bronson didn't want a life without Misty. Misty had used Arlene's car to drive to Beau Carson's house. He'd call Arlene and ask her for Beau's address. If she didn't know, he'd make a few phone calls to some friends until he found out. There was no way Bronson could go another day without telling Misty how he felt. He'd drive all night if he could bring Misty back. The only problem was...would she forgive him?

Outside her window, an overzealous bird sang its morning song before the sun had a chance to rise over the horizon. Misty flipped off the covers, pulled on a thin robe, and made her way to the kitchen to pour a glass of juice. She turned and studied the not-so-familiar surroundings she'd tried to make home—a very masculine oversized kitchen designed for show more than practicality. She was positive most of the appliances hadn't been used. Did Beau even cook? It seemed cold and uninviting.

This wasn't going to work. Beau had left for a weeklong rodeo trip, and she was housesitting at best. As handsome as he was, there was no chemistry between them. It didn't feel right, and she didn't want an *arrangement*; she wanted a family. She missed Crystal Cove, the home she'd grown to love, and her friends. She had the money to repair her home and start up a business. All she had to do was claim it.

She walked outside, the air still and damp in the pre-dawn hours as dew settled over the grassy yard. She pulled her thin robe tighter around her as she sat on the porch and imagined the family life she longed for her baby. A loving mother and a father, not two people joined together out of a sense of obligation. Beau was an impressive guy, just not for her. There were plenty of woman eager to fill her shoes. Sadness made her want to climb back into bed and bury her head under the covers. She stood, about to go back inside, when she noticed a truck with a bright set of headlights driving down the main road that divided Beau's property in half. Had Beau forgotten something? Misty set her almost empty glass on the wooden rail and stared out into the darkness.

The truck approached at a snail's pace, carefully crawling up the road, but there was no way to mistake the golden horseshoe emblem on the side. Misty's heart skipped a beat when she saw who was behind the wheel of the truck.

Bronson! Why was he here? She shivered as he drew closer.

The truck came to a stop right in front of the porch, and he killed the engine. Misty caught her breath, trying not to show an ounce of emotion. Why would he drive all the way out here? She was pretty sure they'd said all they had to say to one another.

Bronson opened the door, stepped out, and reached for something wrapped in a blanket. He carried it in his arms.

"We missed you."

Her heart beat wildly in her chest, and her head scanned a thousand reasons why she should tell him to leave. *We*?

He took a few more steps, removed the wiggling puppy from the blanket in his arms, and set it on the ground. The fluffy little ball of energy looked up and ran over to Misty, wagging its tail. She reached down to pick it up. It was her favorite puppy from the litter. The little pup licked her face while she stroked its silky fur.

"This sweet little girl's named Lucky. I'm hoping she'll bring me luck, so you'll forgive me."

"Forgive you?" Did he understand and forgive her for not confiding in him? Would he be able to accept the baby and Beau in her child's life?

"Carly explained everything. I was so focused on how it affected me that I didn't think of how difficult it must have been for you." He walked up the steps to stand before her with only inches between them. She could smell his masculine woodsy scent. This was who she belonged with. Could they overcome everything that had happened?

Tears began to well up, catching in her lashes. The pain of her mother's abandonment, losing her grandmother, and discovering an unplanned pregnancy came bubbling to the surface. "This isn't how I planned my life, but sometimes life throws you curve balls."

He tilted his head and smiled. "A very wise man told me the same thing." He removed his hat, and set it on the wooden bench nearby. Wrapping her in his arms, he looked deep in her eyes, and she could see for the first time the love she had been longing for.

"Come home with me?" He brushed a strand of hair away from her face and carefully tucked it behind her ear. She realized the sight she must look. She ran her fingers through her hair while balancing the puppy in her other arm.

"Together we can raise this baby, because I can't picture

my life without you." He placed a gentle kiss on her lips. "And I love you beyond measure."

She smiled, blinking away a few tears, and for the first time in her life, she just might have the kind of life she imagined.

"Marry me." It wasn't a question. Lucky licked both their faces as though she wanted to seal the deal and remove any doubts.

Misty nodded and said, "Yes. What about Beau? He's going to be part of the baby's life."

"Don't worry. We'll work it out." When he held her close, she was confident she didn't have to worry as long as they faced their issues together.

He scooped her up in his arms and carried her to the truck. "Now let's go home and plan a wedding."

Debra Fisk

Epilogue

"**A**re you ready?" the doctor asked. Misty looked over at Bronson and smiled as they held hands. Their shiny new wedding bands sparkled like the love in her hearts. She had so much to be thankful for and knew her grandmother would be pleased and smiling down at her.

So much had happened in the past few weeks. She'd returned home with Bronson where they'd had a simple wedding in the small chapel in town. All of Crystal Cove had attended. Misty had squeezed into her grandmother's wedding gown with the help of Darla who made simple alterations to the waistline.

The Florida Barbecue Society had declared Misty Summers the official winner, and she had collected the prize money. She and Bronson were going to work together to create the product line of Summer Heat barbecue sauces and McCabe's Marinades, blending the two names into a full line of products.

Seeing the baby on the screen, she replied, "Yes," excited

she could finally share this moment with the man she loved. Bronson looked as excited as she felt. It was funny how things worked out. Beau had actually sounded relieved when she'd told him she couldn't marry him and that she had left with Bronson. He offered to always be there monetarily for their child but had received a large international endorsement contract that would take him on the road for months at a time. Beau said he would always be a part of their child's life, too, and he would be in touch as soon as he got back in the country.

Bronson decided they should build their own home on his family's land, and while it was under construction, they would stay in Misty's house. Carly had moved in with Darla, wanting to give the newlyweds time to get to know each other better and welcome their new baby when the time came.

"Congratulations to you both. You're having a boy." The doctor beamed as he gave them the news.

"A son," they said in unison.

Misty laughed. She could envision her little cowboy learning to ride with the help of Bronson and his brothers. Her son would have the best of both worlds: loving parents and a collection of uncles to learn from. She really did have a life better than she could ever have imagined.

Dear Readers,

I hope you enjoyed reading Summer Heat. If you would like to connect with me, please contact me at:

Website: www.debrafisk.com
Twitter: @debra_fisk
Facebook:
https://www.facebook.com/debraannfiskauthor/
https://www.facebook.com/debraann.fisk
Pinterest:
https://www.pinterest.com/debbie2580/
Instagram:
https://www.instagram.com/debrafisk/